"You can't have both me and your mistress!"

"I haven't got a mistress!" he said through clenched teeth.

She lifted her chin defiantly, outstaring him, jealousy and pain in her face and voice. "Did you think I'd forgotten about her? Having the baby hasn't softened my brain or made me lose my memory, Ross. You said you hadn't been making love to me because your sister told you not to! But I know the truth, don't I? You haven't been interested in me because you're having an affair with Suzy!"

She's sexy,
successful...
and
PREGNANT!

Relax and enjoy the last in our series of stories
about spirited women and gorgeous men,
whose passion results in pregnancies...
sometimes unexpected! Of course, the birth of
a baby is always a joyful event, and we can
guarantee that our characters will become
besotted moms and dads—but what happened
in those nine months before?

Share the surprises, emotions, dramas and
suspense as our parents-to-be come to terms
with the prospect of bringing a new little life into
the world.... All will discover that the business of
making babies brings with it the most special
love of all....

CHARLOTTE LAMB

The Yuletide Child

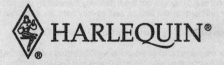

HARLEQUIN®

TORONTO • NEW YORK • LONDON
AMSTERDAM • PARIS • SYDNEY • HAMBURG
STOCKHOLM • ATHENS • TOKYO • MILAN • MADRID
PRAGUE • WARSAW • BUDAPEST • AUCKLAND

ISBN 0-373-12070-2

THE YULETIDE CHILD

First North American Publication 1999.

CHAPTER ONE

ONCE the curtain went up and the music began Dylan lost awareness of everything outside the enchanted circle of light in which she and Michael moved, their bodies in total harmony, gliding sinuously, like snakes, entwining, limb against limb, slithering down each other in erotic invitation, then suddenly breaking apart, whirling away in opposite directions, leaping so high the audience always gasped in disbelief. Not that Dylan heard them.

She heard, saw, nothing but Michael and her own black shadow flying across the white backcloth, the white-painted boards under their feet, until their bodies met once more, writhed in embrace, caressing, imploring, slid to the floor and joined there, rose and fell over and over again, quivering in breathtaking ecstasy.

You could have heard a pin drop in the audience. It was the same every night. The watchers were transfixed and aroused, barely breathing, not moving, until the final second when the two young lovers sank into completed repose.

It wasn't until they took their curtain calls and the thunder of applause broke over them that she began to come out of the hypnotic trance in which she always experienced 'Exercises for Lovers'.

Sweat pouring down her body, shuddering with anguished breath, trembling and exhausted, with Michael holding her hand, supporting her, she looked out into the audience for the first time, curtseying, bending her head in recognition of the audience response.

5

Normally she never noticed anyone out there, but tonight her flickering gaze stopped suddenly as it moved over the rows of faces. She stared into dark eyes in a sort of shock.

He was sitting in the front row of the stalls, leaning forward, his stare glowing and intense, face pale in the shadows, hair black as night. Prince of Darkness, she thought, a little feverish, wildly hyper after the fierce concentration of the dance. That was what he looked like: a creature of the night, a lost soul.

She had never seen him before, yet she felt instantly that she had always known him, that he had haunted her dreams all her life.

Michael felt the shudder which ran through her, and shot her a quick, sideways look.

Turning, lifting her hand to his lips, his lithe body bent in a gesture of adoration, he whispered, 'What's wrong?'

'Nothing, just a ghost walking over my grave,' she lied, and was surprised that she did, because she and Michael knew each other better than anyone else in the world. She had never hidden anything from him before, but she couldn't tell him what had just happened to her; she had no words to describe that weird, out-of-this-world sensation.

The flowers came on, as they always did at this point, cellophane-wrapped bouquets from fans. She and Michael accepted them gracefully, cradled them in the crook of their arms, each blowing a kiss to the audience. It was all a ritual, part of the performance, and she went through it in the same well-rehearsed, smiling fashion.

Tonight was different, though. Tonight she kept looking down into the front row of seats, finding those eyes, and feeling her heart beating right through her until her entire body seemed to be one passionate heartbeat.

What is the matter with me? she thought as Michael led her off, their hands still linked, into the wings, followed by the roar of applause which was like waves beating on a rocky shore. They walked past smiling backstage staff who softly clapped.

'You were wonderful tonight,' a stagehand said.

She smiled mistily. 'Thank you.'

'Beautiful,' their director told them both. 'You just keep getting better, both of you.'

At last they escaped into the quiet, narrow, shadowy corridor which led to the dressing rooms. Only then could she begin to wind down from the heights on which they had danced.

Walking into the square, white-painted box of a room with her name on the door, Dylan sat down on the stool in front of her mirror and blankly gazed at her own reflection: a white-painted face, the face of an icon, not of a human being, a make-up created for this performance by a great make-up artist who had taught her how to renew it quite quickly before every show.

A dew of perspiration showed on the white mask, her painted red mouth was trembling, and under the thickly drawn in black brows her blue eyes were dominated by enlarged pupils like glistening black fruit.

'You sure you're okay?' asked Michael from the door, frowning. 'You aren't sick, are you?'

She could never talk after a performance. She shook her head, managing a smile.

'Sure?'

She nodded.

'Okay, then. See you in twenty minutes?' Michael said, his grey eyes watchful. He looked after her as if she was a child, but for the moment he let it go, closing the door.

She shut her eyes and just sat there, breathing. The relief of being alone was wonderful. Dancing in a spotlight with hundreds of eyes watching you was an ordeal to her, even though she had been doing it now for years. Oh, of course she loved to dance, and the audience response always lifted her, but she always had the fear of making a mistake, stumbling, missing a cue. The tension wound up and up until you thought you would die, and it took time to unwind afterwards.

She slowly began to remove her make-up; underneath it her skin was red and prickly with heat, so she used a handful of gel to soothe as well as cleanse her skin. She had no dresser; she didn't need one. Her costume was very simple, just a flesh-coloured, skintight bodystocking which covered her from her neck to her feet. Seen from the auditorium, it looked as if she was dancing in the nude, which was exactly how Michael wanted it to look.

Dylan slowly and carefully unpeeled the costume, like a snake shedding a slippery skin, then dropped it into a wicker basket. Tomorrow morning it would be put into a washing machine by the wardrobe mistress, spin-dried and hung up ready for tomorrow night's performance.

She always had to dust it inside with talc before she dressed; it was not easy to wriggle into the costume and she had never enjoyed wearing it.

Naked, she walked into her *en suite* bathroom, used the lavatory, which she was never able to do from the moment she put on her costume until she took it off, then had a long, cooling, relaxing shower, taking her time, dried herself and put on clean white panties and a matching bra.

The new dance ate up energy. It was physically demanding; every night she felt limp and drained afterwards. She was shivering now as if she had flu. For some reason tonight was worse than usual.

Because of those eyes, she thought, seeing them again: primitive, disturbing, the glittering eyes of a wolf in the forest, watching, stalking you before it leapt.

Oh, stop being melodramatic! she told herself, laughing at her own imagination as she went back into the dressing room. He was just another fan staring, and wasn't that what Michael wanted from the audience—that fixed intensity of attention on what the dancers on stage were doing?

He was a brilliant choreographer and 'Exercises for Lovers' was the best thing he had created so far. She was very lucky to have met him at ballet school, to have formed a close partnership with him so young that had formed their careers. Their audiences thought of them together...Adams and Carossi...nobody spoke of one without the other. Dylan was a dancer, pure and simple, she had no other ambition—but Michael Carossi had always dreamt of becoming a choreographer, of being the best in the world. Dancing was not enough for him any more, he needed to invent his own steps, create the ballets they danced.

His choreography was intensely physical. Every day they had to rehearse for hours, bending, stretching, doing those incredible leaps, warming muscles to keep their bodies supple during the performance that evening. This was an exhausting ballet; she would be glad when they changed the programme to something less demanding.

The door into the corridor wasn't locked. It was un unwritten rule backstage that if a door was closed you did not open it without knocking first and waiting to be invited in, so she never bothered to lock the door before getting undressed.

Hearing the door opening, she called out, 'I'm getting dressed!' looked into her mirror and felt her heart kick against her ribs.

He stood in the doorway, his dark eyes piercing her like a laser, moving over her slender, pale-skinned, almost naked body, leaving heat everywhere it touched.

Breathlessly, she managed to say, 'Didn't you hear me say I'm getting dressed?'

'No, I didn't. Sorry.' The door shut again.

She was disturbed to find that her hands were trembling as she slid a filmy white slip over her head, smoothing down the delicate straps over her creamy shoulders, a flurry of lace over her breasts. Over that she added a gossamer-fine yellow chiffon dress, tight-waisted, low-necked, full-skirted, which made satisfying swishing noises around her thighs.

She blow-dried her damp hair, brushing the short brown curls into a semblance of order. Michael said the hairstyle made her look like a boy, especially as she had such a skinny, flat, athlete's body.

Outside her door she heard loud, angry voices, and stiffened. What on earth was going on out there?

The door snapped open; Michael appeared in the doorway, his thin, fine-boned face flushed in anger. 'This guy says he's a friend of yours—is that right?'

Over his bony shoulder she met the dark eyes; they pleaded, urged.

'Yes,' she heard herself say, and couldn't believe she had said it, almost contradicted herself, took it back. What on earth was the matter with her, pretending she knew this total stranger?

Of course, if she denied knowing him Michael would

have him thrown out at once—and to her surprise she recognised that she didn't want that to happen. She wanted to get to know this man.

Angrily pushing back a lock of damp, fair hair from his forehead, Michael demanded, 'Who is he?'

Before she could think of a reply the other man answered for her. 'None of your business.' He pushed his way past Michael, closing the door in his face with a cool arrogance that took Dylan's breath away. She had never seen anyone treat Michael Carossi as if he was just any other man. Michael was used to admiration, respect, the heady fumes of hero-worship from the whole company as well as their audiences. Michael was the god of their little world; the whole company revolved around him, including her.

The stranger stood, staring at her, and suddenly the room seemed far too small, she could hardly breathe.

'You look...' he began huskily, then stopped, swallowing; she saw his throat move. 'Beautiful,' he finished.

'Thank you,' she said, dry-mouthed, and forced a pretence of laugher. 'I'm not, though—it's an illusion, especially on stage. It's just the make-up and clothes. I'm really very ordinary.' Her eyes glanced sideways into the dressing table mirror at the slender girl reflected there. Brown hair, a small, heart-shaped face, slightly built—there was nothing special about her. There never had been.

'Ordinary?' he repeated. 'Is that really how you feel? All this glamour, the show business stuff, the fans, the fuss people make over you! Do you wish you were just an ordinary girl?'

'But that's what I am! An ordinary girl who happens to be able to dance.'

'You must have wanted to be a dancer!'

'It just happened to me. I started when I was four years old, taking dancing lessons once a week. All my mother's idea, actually. I don't remember ever wanting to; it was all so long ago. I had no idea where it would all end. Nobody warns you that if you go on with it you'll spend endless days in punishing, gruelling work. They don't tell you about the muscle strain, the agony of sore feet, the aching back...' She broke off, surprised by what she was telling him, flushed and worried. If he turned out to be a journalist and published what she had just said Michael would be furious with her! Hurriedly, she asked, 'Look, who are you? How did you get in here?'

'Walked in,' he calmly said.

'The stage doorkeeper should have stopped you!' As if poor old George would have had much chance of keeping him out!

Nearly sixty, a cheerful, grey-haired man who had been a dancer once, George had broken a leg when he was thirty and never danced again. He had been given a job backstage and had graduated through various jobs to doorkeeper. Wiry, with a faint limp even now, George was practical and kind-hearted, a father-figure to the young dancers, but he would never be able to deal with a man like this.

The tough mouth curled up at one edge. 'He was busy on the phone; he didn't see me!'

Preferred not to, no doubt! thought Dylan. George had a strong sense of self-preservation; he wouldn't risk getting his head knocked off!

Her blue eyes absorbed everything about the stranger, starting with that mouth. Wide, passionate, beautifully moulded, it had an erotic power that made her quiver.

The very idea of being kissed by him made her head swim.

How tall was he? A foot taller than her; her head just came up to his wide shoulders. Now that he was under the raw glare of her dressing room lights she could see that he was not pale at all; no doubt it had been the contrast of his black hair and paler skin in shadows. In fact he was deeply tanned, brown as a berry, and very fit. A lean man, with a lot of muscles under that white shirt. Those stark, angular cheekbones, that strong jaw-line, made him a man any woman would find compelling and any man would find a threat.

'What's your name?'

He smiled and her ears beat with a hot pulse. 'Ross Jefferson. Is Dylan Adams your real name?'

She nodded. 'What do you do? You aren't in the theatre, are you?' He looked as if he spent all his time out of doors, but then she, of all people, knew how deceptive appearances could be!

'No, I am not,' he said, grimacing. 'I'm a forester—I work in a commercially managed forest, way up north—all conifers, of course.'

She gave a sigh of relief—at least he wasn't a journalist looking for a gossip story!

'I had a holiday in Norway once, when I was at school. There were forests of fir trees everywhere we went.' They were making polite conversation on the surface but underneath something very different was happening. She barely knew what she was saying, she was so intent on what she was feeling: a sensuality which was entirely new to her and left her in a state of shock.

She had had a few boyfriends in the past, but her career took first place in her life; there wasn't time to get seriously involved with anyone. Except Michael, of course; he was always there. They saw each other every day, most of their waking hours, but their relationship was not a sexual one. They were more than friends, less than lovers. Partners, necessary to each other on stage and off, working together, eating together, spending their spare time together. How could she ever have fallen in love with anyone else? Michael left no room for any other man.

At that instant, right on cue, Michael tapped on the door. 'Are you coming, Dylan? I'm not waiting much longer; I'm starving. Come on!'

'Will you have supper with me?' Ross Jefferson quickly asked.

'I always eat with Michael after a performance.'

His eyes focused on hers intently, his face hard, set. 'Are you two lovers?'

The direct, flat question made her flush.

'No, just very good friends.' Yet more than that; the answer was too simplistic. What else could she say, though? There were no words to describe how close she and Michael were.

'Then eat with me tonight!' Ross said urgently, moving closer to her, but not touching her. 'I want to get to know you. I'm only in London for a week. I'm here on holiday and have to get back to work by next Monday, at the other end of the country. God knows when I shall be able to come to London again. I've no time to waste.'

'Dylan!' Michael shouted again. 'Our table is booked for eleven! Come on!'

Still staring into the dark, hypnotic eyes, Dylan called out, 'You go on without me, Michael. See you tomorrow at rehearsal.'

A silence, then the door was pulled open and Michael stared in at her, at both of them. There was incredulity, alarm, wariness in his elegant face. This had never happened before. She had never shown any sign of preferring another man's company to his. Something new had entered their magic circle, something dangerous to Michael, and he immediately sensed it. He had powerful intuitions, especially where his own security was involved.

'I need to talk over tonight's performance. It won't wait.'

'I'm sorry,' she said, meaning far more than that she was sorry she couldn't eat supper with him. She was saying she was sorry she wouldn't be able to talk through the way they had danced, analyse any mistakes, discuss the audience reaction to this movement or that, the way they always did after each performance, while it was fresh in their minds. Each night was so different, each audience responded differently; you learnt so much from studying them. Added to all that, they had to talk themselves down from the fierce excitement of the night.

And tonight Dylan was changing all that. Tonight Michael was no longer the centre of her universe. A new element had entered the equasion.

'I'm having supper with Ross,' she said.

Michael stood there, very still, intensely concentrated on her, staring into her eyes and reading everything in them.

They knew each other so well. She couldn't hide anything from him. She didn't even try.

'I'll talk to you tomorrow,' he said at last. The door slammed again; he was gone but she was trembling.

Ross stared at the door, then down at her; she stiffened, waiting for him to question her again about Michael. His eyes were hard and narrowed, dark with thought, but all he said was, 'Shall we get away before he comes back to argue some more? My car's parked in the next street.'

The fans were outside the stage door, clustered around Michael, who was signing autographs. Ross took her hand and hurried her away, around the corner, before they were noticed. The crowds had all gone now. The streets were silent; their footsteps rang out in the stillness. This part of London did not have as much traffic at night as the busier parts of town. It was mostly city offices, very few people worked at night around here, and the shops and restaurants were all closed. The air was warm, a faint breeze blew her silky skirts around her legs.

'Where are we going to eat?'

'You suggest somewhere.'

'I know an Italian trattoria not far from here—they stay open until midnight. Do you like Italian food?'

'Love it.' He stopped walking, looked down at her. 'I don't believe this,' he said abruptly, still holding her hand. Raising it to his chest, he splayed it over his shirt-front. 'Can you feel my heart beating?'

Her palm flattened, she stood still, the heavy thudding right under her warm skin, and nodded, unable to speak.

Ross looked at her with a passion that made her quiver. 'Do you feel it, too? It's as if I've been struck by lightning. I think I've fallen in love with you at first sight, and I never even believed in such a thing.'

'Me, too,' she whispered, and then he bent his head, his warm mouth moving against hers, sending the world whirling crazily around them.

They spent the next two hours talking in a corner of the trattoria, eating their way through melon and prosciutto, the swordfish cooked in tomatoes, olives and garlic, with a green salad, followed by green figs.

'Are you dieting?' he asked her, and she laughed.

'I don't need to—I use up so much energy every day. I'm underweight for my height. But I love swordfish, don't you?'

'I've never eaten it before, but it's good. Tell me about your usual day. When do you get up? Can we have breakfast together?'

'You're going too fast!'

'I have to—there isn't time to take it slowly. I live hundreds of miles away and I don't get much time off.'

He told her about his forest, talking passionately about his trees, how he worked among them, the life he led in the northern area between England and Scotland which was his home.

She told him how hard and fiercely she had to work each day, how much she loved to dance, but how tired she often was.

He asked her again about Michael. 'Has he ever been your lover? Is he in love with you?'

'No,' she said to both questions.

'Don't tell me you're just good friends! He's far too possessive for that to be true!'

'We're partners. It's hard to explain. We need each other. It isn't love.' Nothing so easy to define, nothing so simple. Michael threatened the back of her mind like a bruise, darkening her skin, worrying her. How would he reaact to what was happening to her?

'Never has been?' insisted Ross, and she shook her head.

'No. Michael has girlfriends but I was never one of them.'

'Were there other men in your life?'

'Nobody special. There was never enough time. I had to work too hard and I was always tired.'

Ross drove her back to her flat in Islington, just a mile away from the theatre.

'I won't ask you in; it's gone one o'clock, and I have to get some sleep,' she said, sitting in his car outside the building.

'Breakfast...when?' He was very close. She knew he was going to kiss her; she was dying for the touch of his mouth. She couldn't think about anything else. 'Eight o'clock?'

'Nine! I've got rehearsals at eleven,' she thought aloud, knowing that tomorrow she was going to regret losing so much sleep. She needed a solid eight hours every night to restore her energy levels, so that she could keep up with her demanding schedule.

'Skip them and spend the day with me.'

'I can't, Michael would kill me. We have to work at the barre every day to keep supple; muscles stiffen up so quickly if you don't.'

'When can you get away, then?'

'Lunchtime. One o'clock. Then I'm supposed to have a rest, a nap before the evening performance. I don't get much free time.'

'Breakfast and then lunch,' he said, framing her face between his hands and bending.

Their mouths clung; she felt heat deep inside her body. It was the first time in her entire life that she had ever wanted a man like that.

A week later they got engaged. The wedding was fixed for a month after that, although her father almost had kittens when she said she was planning to marry so quickly. Her mother would have been dead for two years that spring; it seemed longer. Dylan still missed her and wished she could talk to her about Ross, about getting married. Ingrid Adams had been fifty the year she'd died of cancer, after a mercifully short illness. Dylan's father, Joe Adams, still hadn't quite got over it, and was unable to cope with organising a wedding.

'There isn't time! You can't arrange a wedding this soon!' he said to her helplessly. 'Why not wait a few months, give yourself time to think, time for us to organise everything?'

'We don't want to wait. We just want to get married!'

He looked at her sister, Jenny, throwing up his hands in despair. Jenny tried to argue her out of being in such a hurry, too, but gave up when she realized Dylan simply was not listening.

Michael was worse. Michael went crazy, white and shaking, his eyes black holes in his head. 'You can't do this to me—you can't chuck everything away. For pity's sake, Dylan, it's just infatuation. Sleep with him, but don't marry him. How can you go on with your career if you live at the back of beyond? You have to be in London to dance.'

'I'm sorry, Michael,' was all she could say, almost in tears herself, because she hated quarrelling with him. She felt guilty because what he had said was true. She wasn't just getting married. She was giving up her career. She was walking away from Michael and everything they had built up together.

'My contract ends this month; I'm not signing up again.' Their season ended, too, at the same time; they would have gone into rehearsal for a month, then gone on a protracted tour of the States before returning in the autumn to open a new season here in London. Now Michael would be doing all that without her.

Michael grabbed her shoulders and shook her, hoarsely shouting. 'I won't let you do it! What about me? What am I supposed to do? I can't dance without you.'

He made her nervous, but she lifted her chin to stare back at him defiantly. 'I'm sorry, Michael. Don't be so angry. I know it's going to be a problem, but it will be a challenge, too—can't you see that? You'll find a new partner; they'll queue up for the chance to dance with you, you know that. I'm not unique. You'll find someone else, just as good, probably even better, and go on to even greater heights.'

His face was stormy, full of bitterness. 'What's the matter with you? You're a great dancer, arguably the best of our generation…you can't throw it all away on this stupid, ordinary, boring guy. My God, Dylan—he's nobody. He doesn't even understand what you are, how wonderful you are. He knows nothing about ballet. He is destroying a great dancer without even knowing what a great dancer is!'

Helplessly she pleaded for him to understand, her voice shaking 'Michael, try to see it from our side—he loves me: we love each other.'

'Stop saying that—I just told you, it won't last for ever; it never does. Use your brain, Dylan. What the hell is wrong with you? You're possessed…out of your mind, crazy.'

She laughed nervously. 'Maybe I am, but there's nothing I can do about it. I am being driven, Michael. I can't think of anything else but Ross. If I stayed on in the ballet I'd be worse than useless. It doesn't seem important any more. I no longer want to dance.'

He looked as shocked as if she had hit him in the face. 'You can't be serious. I'd rather see you dead at my feet than let you stop dancing. The idea is unthinkable. You were born to dance, and I won't let you stop, do you hear me? You aren't going to do it!'

'Yes, I am, Michael.'

It went on day after day, all the same arguments, the same pleas and angry protests, until her wedding day.

Michael's bitterness and rage made life impossible in the theatre during that month but Dylan rode the storm somehow, her mind entirely set on the moment when she would become Ross's wife. Michael was right—she was possessed, nothing else mattered to her, she was being carried away by an instinct older than time. She wanted to sleep in Ross's bed every night, bear his children, spend her life with him. The life force had her in its grip and her career no longer mattered a damn. She found rehearsing tiring; the nightly performances passed in a vague dream. She was no longer part of the company. In her own mind she had already left, although her body went on performing.

She hadn't believed Michael would come to the wedding, but he did, glowering darkly from his seat in the church. His friends, the company, all the dancers they had been to school with, were on his side, their eyes accusing her of treachery, betrayal. How could she do this to him? they silently asked, those eyes.

Afterwards, at the reception, he walked up to Dylan in her white dress and veil. She stiffened, afraid of what he might do next, but all he did was take her hands and kiss them lingeringly, the backs and then the pale pink palms.

'I'm not saying goodbye. You'll be back. You can't exist away from us. When the madness passes, you'll come back to me.'

'Don't hold your breath, Carossi!' Ross snapped,

tense as a drawn bow beside her, putting his arm around her waist and pulling her close to him.

Michael ignored him as if he was invisible. Dylan watched him walk away, sadness welling up inside her. Ever since they'd first met at ballet school they had been so close, almost one person instead of two; it was hard to say goodbye, harder to think of life without him.

She and Ross left for their honeymoon a few minutes later. They flew to Italy and spent two weeks at a small hotel in the Tuscan hills, making love day and night with a passion that excluded everyone and everything else, although they managed to spend a day at Venice and another at Florence. Dylan remembered both days like waking dreams: she and Ross wandered together, entranced, through the cities, looking at each other, not the beautiful buildings, the River Arno, the Grand Canal, the famous paintings, the statues in the narrow, old streets of both those ancient and exquisite cities. They were merely the background of the happiness Dylan and Ross shared, like painted designs on a stage backcloth.

After their honeymoon Ross took her up north to the house they were going to share, and for the first time she saw his forest, the ranked dark green of the conifers, the scent of pine, the darkness in the heart of the trees. There was no other house in sight. There was very little traffic; few cars ever passed along that narrow road.

Dylan was a city girl, used to the busy streets of London, the noise and fumes, the roofs crowding the skyline, other people everywhere. Even during their honeymoon there had always been crowds circling them. Now they were alone, in a haunted landscape.

This was the first moment she felt a stirring of doubt, a sense of panic. She had married Ross without stopping to think about what she was throwing away, leaving behind; the city she had lived in all her life, the pleasure and pain of dancing, the companionship of the ballet company, the partnership with Michael which had been her life for years.

From her first sight of Ross none of that had seemed to matter any more. She had become a driven creature, only knowing she needed this man more than breath itself. Love had not so much obsessed her as consumed her, taken over her whole life.

Now she was alone with Ross and his forest, facing the consequences of her marriage, looking down into the deep abyss between her past and her future, the life she had led and the life she would lead in future. Standing at the window of their bedroom, looking out, she saw nothing but trees and sky, heard only the wind moving the branches, the sigh and whisper of the forest, and fear prickled under her skin.

What had she done?

CHAPTER TWO

AND then Ross came up behind her, put his arms around her waist and kissed her softly on the side of her neck. Dylan leaned back against him, sighing with pleasure, pushing away her moment of doubt and uncertainty. She loved him more than she had ever loved anything or anyone else before. Whatever she had had to give up weighed very little in the scales against having Ross.

'Come and meet my trees,' he whispered.

He always talked about them as if they were human, had feelings, could hear what he said to them and even answered him in their own way. Dylan smiled, touched by that, by his passionate commitment to his work That was what she wanted from him—that deep, unfaltering love. She wanted to give as much back, too.

'I'm dying to!' she assured him.

His smile of pleasure made her heart lift. He wanted her to share his feelings about the forest. Dylan wanted to be part of every aspect of his life. Wasn't that what marriage meant? Sharing everything, becoming one flesh, one heart, one mind?

The unforgettable scent of pine met them as soon as they walked through the gate in their garden hedge into the forest. Ferns brushed their legs, flies and midges buzzed them, powdery-winged brown and blue butter-flies hovered over spring flowers in the long grass at the forest rim. Under their feet was the crunch of pine nee-dles. Sunlight laid out needle-fine paths in front of them under the fir trees until they faded into darkness.

As the shadows around them deepened Dylan couldn't help shivering. 'It's quite cold in here, isn't it?'

She was wearing jeans and a light pink shirt, over which she wore a denim waistcoat but no jacket because the weather was warm for late March, so long as you were out in the sunlight. Once they were deep into the forest, though, the sun didn't penetrate the closely set trees and her skin had chilled rapidly.

Ross gave her a quick look, then took off his tweed jacket and put it round her shoulders. 'Better?'

She snuggled into the warmth from his body which the tweed retained along with his own particular body scent. 'That's lovely. But I don't want you to get cold. Maybe we should go back?'

'Oh, I'm used to working out here in all weathers; I never feel the cold.' He took her hand. 'Come on, I want to show you something.'

She had to move quickly to keep up with his long-legged stride. The tall pines stretched all around them now; they were deep into the forest, with very little light to show them where they were going, and Dylan was oddly afraid of the pressing tree trunks, the shadows, the cool, pine-scented air.

All the forests and woods she had ever known had had broadleaf trees, oak and hornbeam, beech and ash, which shed their leaves in autumn and did not grow too close together, so that open glades stretched in places, full of light and giving space for wild flowers and tussocks of long grass. She had never been nervous in those woods, but she was nervous now.

At last Ross stopped moving and put a finger to his lips, whispering to her, 'Keep very still. Look...there...' He pointed to a tree a few feet away.

Obediently not moving, Dylan peered, but at first

could not see anything interesting. Then there was a shirr of wings, a flash of gold and cream. A tiny bird flew up to a branch of the conifer and perched on a web of ivy. A second later Dylan spotted a basket-shape hanging there; the little bird disappeared into it.

Looking up at Ross, she silently shaped the word 'nest'.

He nodded. 'A goldcrest's nest,' he whispered, so softly she could only just hear him.

The bird flew out and vanished among the trees, and Ross said very quietly, 'The nest is made of moss—isn't it clever, the way it's made? She must have fledglings. We often get goldcrests here; they feed on insects which live on conifers, breed in the bark—beetles and flies, for instance—not many birds live among fir trees, but it's a habitat that agrees with goldcrests.'

'I've never seen a goldcrest before,' she said wonderingly. 'It's such a wonderful colour.'

'No, you wouldn't have—they aren't city birds.'

'I wish I could see the fledglings. Do you know, I've never seen a bird's nest? If I'd had a brother I might have done, but there was just me and Jenny and we never went bird-nesting.'

'I'm glad to hear it—these days it's very frowned on. You're encouraged to use binoculars and watch a nest, never to interfere with it, and certainly never to remove eggs.'

'Do people still do that?'

'Unfortunately, yes. Some collectors have no conscience. Luckily, that tree is far too high to climb. Goldcrests aren't common birds; we have to protect them.' Glancing at his watch, he said, 'Look at the time! We've been in here nearly an hour. Doesn't time fly when you're enjoying yourself? We'd better start walking back.'

Dylan was relieved to see the sunlit edge of the forest reappearing. There was something disturbing about the deep interior of the forest; it was so silent and full of shadows, making the skin on the back of her neck creep. She couldn't say why, except that, perhaps, she knew so little about the natural world. She had lived in a great city all her life. She had a lot to learn.

Just before they left the forest something red flashed up a tree, making her jump and stand still, staring upward.

'What was that?'

'A red squirrel,' Ross said casually.

Her eyes widened. 'Red? I've never seen a red one; in London we only have grey squirrels.' She stood staring up the tree; the squirrel peered down at her, its bushy tail flicking to and fro. 'Will it come if I feed it some nuts? There were squirrels in the park near where I lived which came right up to you and took nuts from your hand.'

'They were semi-tame—this is a wild squirrel,' Ross told her. 'It might run down and snatch nuts if you threw them and stayed back, but it wouldn't eat out of your hand.'

As they finally left the forest, coming out into the sunlight, she asked him, 'Have you got any books I could read? On the forest?'

'I'll find one for you,' Ross promised. 'And this evening, after supper, we'll take another walk. I'll show you the moths; they are really something! The forest is very different at night.'

Dylan hoped he didn't notice the atavistic shudder running through her at the idea of going into the forest in the dark. Smiling bravely, she said, 'Wonderful, I'll look forward to that.' Somehow she had to learn to love the forest for his sake.

They never got very far among the trees that night, though. Before they had gone more than a few steps Dylan felt something scuttle across her face and screamed, frantically brushing her skin to get rid of whatever it was.

Ross had a torch in one hand; he switched it on and turned it on her, blinding her. 'Stand still. Oh, it's just a spider.' He flicked one finger. 'There, it's gone. It was a wolf spider.'

Shuddering, she said, 'A wolf spider? Why is it called that? Does it bite?'

Ross switched off his torch and put both arms round her, pulling her close to him, kissing her hair. 'Of course not. Are you scared of spiders? There's no need to be; there are no poisonous spiders in Britain. Wolf spiders hunt their prey instead of just sitting in a web waiting for it. And they eat other insects, not people!'

'How was I to know that? I'm not up on spiders.' She tried to laugh, lifting her face, and saw his eyes gleaming in the shadows. 'Even you seem strange,' she whispered. 'I don't know you out here, in the dark.'

'Then I'll have to remind you who I am,' he murmured thickly, his head coming down.

His mouth blotted out memory. She was lost at once, kissing him back passionately, her knees giving. Sliding her arms around his neck, she held him tightly, pressing closer, her body moulding itself to his.

Ross pulled her down into the long, whispering ferns and grass, the scent of the earth and the pines making her head swim. Without breaking off their kiss, they hurriedly began undressing each other with shaky hands.

Dylan buried her flushed, feverish face in his naked chest, groaning with desire, her lips open on his skin.

'I want you so much.'

'Not as much as I want you,' he muttered, sliding on top of her, and her breath exhaled in a strangled gasp as he parted her thighs.

'Darling...oh, darling...'

Her arms around his back, she caught him between her thighs, arching up to meet that first, deep thrust. The need intensified into a frenzy as they moved together, their bodies totally entwined, riding fiercely towards the same intense pleasure.

Their deep moans of satisfaction floated up between the trees into the dark night sky. Afterwards they lay sleepily on their crushed bed of fern, still closely twined, his arm under her, her leg curled across him, staring up into the shadows where pale moths flitted, glistening with powdered wings.

'I love your moths,' she whispered, drowsily wondering how she could ever have felt uncertain about having married him. She had never been so happy in her entire life. It would be wonderful to sleep out here all night, naked in this forest, under the stars and moon, with the scents and sounds of the earth all around them.

Next day he was up at first light while she was still asleep. He woke her with a cup of tea and a slice of buttered toast before he left for work. Drowsily, she blinked up at him, sunlight on her lashes.

He groaned, bending to kiss the warm valley between her breasts. 'I wish I didn't have to go to work. You're far too tempting in that nightie. Even sexier without it, of course.' He pushed the deep lace neckline aside and buried his face against her breasts. 'Mmm...you smell of honey and flowers.'

She stroked his dark hair, ran her fingertips into it, caressed the nape of his neck.

'Get back in bed, Ross, I want you.' She pulled him down closer and he laughed throatily.

'I wish I could, believe me—but I can't. We're back in the real world and I have a job to do.' Straightening, he sighed. 'Got to go, darling. I can't be sure what time I'll be back, but there's plenty of food in the freezer and the fridge. You've got my mobile number if you need me. I'll have to take the car—I'll need it to get from one part of the forest to another, with all my equipment and tools—but if you want to go into the village it's only a couple of miles to walk, or you can get a lift there with the postman if he comes today. He often gives people lifts. Then you'll only have the walk back to face.'

The distance didn't bother her; she would enjoy a walk. 'The exercise will be good for me. I don't want to lose muscle tone. I have to keep supple, and walking is a very good way of doing that.'

'I'll help you keep supple—I can think of some very enjoyable exercises to do every night.'

She giggled. 'I bet you can.'

'When did you say your brother-in-law was going to deliver that object you call a car up here?'

'Don't make fun of my flower wagon! I love it. It may not go very fast but it is reliable, and it's a thing of beauty! A one-off, unique. People always stare when I go by in it.'

'I bet they do,' Ross said curtly.

She had bought it secondhand from a car auction two years ago: a Mini car painted a metallic green. Michael had transformed it over a couple of weekends, painting a jungle all over it—palms and huge, exotic tropical flowers in extraordinary colours.

'Phil hopes to bring it up here next weekend. He can't get the time off during the week. He'll have to take the train to London to pick up my car, then drive it up here and take the train back home to Penrith. It's a long journey; it's very good of Phil to offer to do it.'

Ross nodded. 'Nice guy, Phil. I liked him.'

The emphasis reminded her that he did not like Michael, and never would. She suppressed a faint sigh. If only they could be friends. They were the two most important men in her life and she hated knowing that they resented each other.

'And your sister's nearly as gorgeous as you are,' Ross added, smiling, then looked at his watch. 'Must rush. See you, darling. Oh, and I left a couple of books on the forest for you, on the kitchen table.'

It was her first day alone in the house. She got up after she had finished her toast and tea, showered and dressed in jeans and a loose dark pink shirt, then sat down at the kitchen table and worked out a daily schedule for her housework. She had learned discipline in ballet school; you had to be organised or you got nowhere.

After making their bed and tidying the bedroom and all the rooms downstairs she went out into the garden to gather vegetables for supper. She would make a vegetable casserole, she decided, a layered dish of thick slices of carrots, potatoes, onions, parsnips, turnips and young broad beans. It was a meal she had often cooked before, in London, but there she had used vegetables from a nearby street market. They had not been as fresh as the ones she was picking from Ross's neat, straight rows.

When it was nearly cooked she would stir in tomatoes and mushrooms and sprinkle the top with mixed fresh breadcrumbs and grated cheese to make a crunchy gold topping. She would serve lamb with it for Ross, but she, herself, would only eat the vegetable casserole. As well as exercising daily she would need to diet. For years she had been working out for hours every day, using up a lot of calories and energy. Now that she had stopped she would put on weight if she didn't watch it.

Looking at her watch, she was shaken to see that it was only eleven! The day was dragging. What if Ross didn't get back until six or seven? How was she going to cope with such long days alone, with nothing to do and nobody to talk to?

She left the trug of vegetables on the draining board, to wash later, and made some black coffee. While she drank a cup she sat down at the kitchen table and opened one of the books Ross had left her. It was easier to read than she had been afraid it would be—almost every page had a coloured picture on it and the text was direct and simple. She started with a section on the wildlife of a conifer forest, and read for twenty minutes with deep interest until she suddenly heard Ross's voice outside.

Dropping the book, she rushed to open the front door, then stopped dead as she realised he was not alone. There was a woman in his arms.

Shocked, Dylan froze, staring—who on earth was she? Someone very sophisticated, with blonde hair the colour of a new-hatched chick and a figure with more curves than a switchback ride. Her high, round breasts were shown off by a tight white sweater which clung to every seductive inch, her slim waist was cinched by a black leather belt, and she had very long legs in tight jeans.

Ross turned to smile, his manner unworried and confident. 'Dylan, this is Suzy Hale. She's Alan's wife— I've told you about him, one of my colleagues and a very good friend of mine—they live ten miles off. She's

come along to introduce herself and invite us both over
for dinner, next week. Isn't that nice of her?'

Dylan barely heard half he said. She was too busy
noticing the smear of bright red lipstick on the corner of
his mouth. Did he always kiss his best friend's wife on
the lips?

Somehow, though, she managed a smile and murmured, 'That would be lovely.'

The blonde slid out of Ross's grasp and came towards
her, holding out her hand, the fingers tipped with bright
red nail varnish that matched her lipstick.

'Hi, Dylan, welcome to the back of beyond!' Her fingers were firm and warm and her smile was so friendly
Dylan couldn't help smiling back.

'That's a London accent, isn't it?'

The other woman laughed, her head flung back. 'Well
spotted! I was born in Finchley, lived there for years.
Bit of a culture shock, this place, isn't it, to a Londoner?
How is the old place? I bet you're missing it already! I
know I do. I rarely get a chance to go there since my
family moved to Wales. My brother got a job in a hospital in Cardiff; he's a physiotherapist. Our parents decided to go, too. My father came from Cardiff originally,
so they were keen to go back there. Now I have to stay
in a hotel if I go to London, and, as you know only too
well, London hotels cost an arm and a leg. But then
everything in London is expensive, and on Alan's salary
we can't afford to spend money like a drunken sailor.'
Dylan was dazed by the speed at which the other woman
talked. Scarcely drawing breath, Suzy went on, 'Ross
says you were a ballet dancer—I'm ashamed to admit
I've never ever seen ballet. The only dancing I ever did
was at a rave. I'm not an intellectual, I'm afraid.' She
turned a laughing face at Ross. 'And I can't believe Ross

went to the ballet! Buy the ticket by mistake, did you, Ross? Thought you'd be seeing something like the Folies Bergère?'

Ross seemed very amused by her—did he enjoy her bubbly personality and headlong chatter? Dylan wished she was an extrovert, could talk as easily, but she found it impossible to shed her inhibitions.

Dancing was a physical art; she never needed to talk. She could express herself eloquently in gesture and movement, so she was never self-conscious on a stage, but faced with other people she felt herself tighten up, unable to relax.

'Actually, I bought a ticket because I saw a big blown-up photo of Dylan outside the theatre,' Ross said, and Dylan did a double-take. He had never told her that. He glanced at her, dark grey eyes teasing.

'I knew it! You didn't go in to see a ballet, you went to see more of Dylan. Did she look sexy in a tutu?' Suzy roared with laughter.

'I'm sure she would—but in the photo it looked as if she wasn't wearing anything at all,' Ross drawled. 'She looked totally naked, but when she appeared on stage I realised she was actually wearing a body-stocking.'

Dylan went pink. Was that really why he had come to the ballet that first night? In the hope of seeing her dance in the nude?

'I bet that was a disappointment!' Suzy mocked, and he grinned at her.

'You've got a wicked mind!' He glanced at his watch. 'Look, Dylan, I have an hour to spare. I've finished all the work I need to do this morning, so I popped home to see how you were getting on. I thought maybe we could have an early lunch? Sandwiches and coffee? That won't take you long, will it? Suzy, you'll stay, won't you?'

Politely Dylan said, 'Yes, please stay, Suzy. It won't take me a minute to make some sandwiches, or would you rather have pasta? I could make a quick spaghetti with tomato and basil sauce.'

'Don't tempt me!' Suzy groaned. 'Could you make me a salad sandwich with no butter in it? I'm dieting.'

'Me, too,' Dylan said ruefully. 'How about you, Ross?'

'Cheese, onion and tomato sandwich for me, darling.'

'Okay, I won't be long.' She went off to the kitchen while Ross showed Suzy into the sitting room. While she cut bread, made the salad filling, sliced Ross's favourite Cheddar cheese, she kept thinking about that lipstick on Ross's mouth.

Had that kiss meant anything? But there had been no trace of self-consciousness or secrecy in their behaviour when she appeared. Suzy was just the type who kissed her friends, male or female.

Dylan hoped so. Jealousy was new to her; she never wanted to feel it again, the stab of agony that had pierced her when she first saw the blonde woman in Ross's arms.

When she carried the tray of sandwiches and coffee through she found Ross and Suzy sitting close together on a couch. For a second Dylan felt the sting of jealousy again, then she saw that they were glancing through an album of wedding photos which Dylan's sister had made and sent to them.

'They're quite alike, aren't they, Dylan and her sister?' Suzy was saying.

'There is a resemblance,' Ross agreed. 'But Dylan's beautiful and Jenny is only attractive.'

Dylan's heart turned over—did he really think she was

beautiful? Oh, he had said it to her, when they were making love, but this was the first time she had ever heard him say it to someone else.

Her hands trembled; the china rattled on the tray and he and Suzy looked round. Hurriedly Dylan came forward to put the tray down on a low coffee table.

'Just looking at your wedding pictures,' Suzy told her. 'You made a lovely bride.' Then she leaned over the album again, staring at one photo, and gave a low, throaty gasp. 'Who is *that*? He's the sexiest thing I've seen for years—look at those smouldering eyes! Talk about a turn-on!'

Before she looked down at the photo Dylan knew who it was—who else could it be but Michael, lithe and supple in the dark grey suit he had worn for the wedding? The photo had been taken as the guests arrived for the service. All around him were happy, smiling faces, but the photographer had caught him in grim, bitter mood, glowering at the camera.

Ross glanced at it, scowling. 'Oh, him! He's a ballet dancer.'

Suzy groaned. 'You're kidding? He oozes machismo! But he's gay, I suppose? They always are, aren't they? What a waste!'

Dylan opened her mouth to contradict her, explain that male dancers were no more likely to be gay than the female ones, but Ross talked over her curtly. 'Is that my sandwich, Dylan? I'd better eat it and go. I'm meeting my boss in half an hour. I'll take my coffee black, thanks. What about you, Suzy?'

'Black for me, too, thank you. Are these my sandwiches? They look terrific; I'm starving!'

'Yes, I hope they're okay,' Dylan said, handing her the plate.

Suzy bent her head over them, inhaling. 'They smell wonderful. I love the smell of fresh salad, don't you? Did you grow all this, Ross? He's a great gardener, isn't he, Dylan? I envy you those rows and rows of vegetables. He plants them the way he plants his saplings—straight as a die! Vegetables taste so much better when they've just come out of the garden, don't you agree?'

It was only later, when Ross had gone off back to work and Suzy had set off for her own home, that Dylan remembered that she had never set Suzy right about Michael's sexual orientation. Next time she had a chance she must do so, but she would make certain Ross wasn't in earshot. He hated her to mention Michael, which was typical of a man. He saw nothing wrong in laughing, teasing, almost flirting with Suzy, yet he turned nasty if Michael was mentioned. One law for him, another for her, apparently. Dylan resented that. How would he like it if she started sulking or flying into a rage every time he spoke to Suzy?

The following Friday night there was a bad spring storm in the region; all night long the wind howled around the house. Dylan anxiously watched the trees on the forest edge swaying and bending, and heard on the TV news that houses had suffered serious damage, losing tiles or chimneys, while power lines were brought down and trees toppled. Anxiety kept her awake half the night, but towards dawn the winds died down and she fell into a deep sleep, only to be awoken by the shrilling of the telephone.

Ross moaned something and rolled over to pick up the phone. Sleepily, half believing she was still dreaming, Dylan heard him groan.

'You're kidding? Completely blocked? Yes, we'll

have to deal with that at once. Of course. I'll be there. Okay, Alan. See you in half an hour.'

'What's wrong?' Dylan asked, struggling up in the warm bed as he hung up and started to get out of bed.

'The storm brought down half a dozen trees in Alan's section of the forest. A couple of them have blocked a road, and people are having to make a big detour. The police rang Alan, asking him to get the road cleared as soon as possible. He can't do it on his own; he'll need help. Sorry, darling. I had hoped we could go out somewhere today, but we'll have to put that off until tomorrow. I may be busy most of the day.'

She tried to hide her disappointment. 'Oh, well, maybe we could do something special tomorrow! I'll get up and make your breakfast.'

'No, don't bother, darling. I'll just have a cup of tea and a piece of toast.' He gathered up his clothes and went off to the bathroom, telling her, 'You stay in bed. Try to get some more sleep.'

That was impossible, of course! she lay listening to the sound of the shower, then a few moments later his quiet footsteps on the stairs, the muted movements in the kitchen. She was still wide awake when Ross left. Dylan heard the front door close quietly, the engine of his four-wheel drive start up, then the sound of him driving away, fast.

For another half an hour she lay listening to the empty house; clocks ticked, floorboards creaked, electricity hummed, but she was all alone. Gulls pattered on the roof; they must have flown inland to escape the storm. In a line of thornbeams at the back of the garden rooks sat on their rough nest, squawking and arguing.

Further away, she heard the rustling and whispering

of the forest; the wind had died down but it was still blowing among the branches.

The house was immaculate. She had nothing to do and all day to do it in, alone. Turning over, sobbing, she longed for London, for streets noisy with traffic and people, for the comfort and reassurance of being surrounded by others.

She would have liked to ring her sister, but Jenny would think she was nagging for Phil to go to London and collect her car, and Dylan didn't want her to feel pressured. Saturday was a family day—they all did things together, went shopping, went to the library, had lunch out at some favourite country pub, took the kids cycling on safe country roads, went sailing or walking. So Phil would probably be bringing her car tomorrow.

Dylan wished, though, that he was coming today— bringing Jenny and the kids with him. That would have been something to look forward to; it would have brightened the whole weekend.

Sighing, she got out of bed and began the usual dull routine of showering, dressing in jeans and a shirt, tidying the bedroom, collecting the clothes she and Ross had worn yesterday, taking them downstairs to go into the washing machine. Within half an hour she had eaten breakfast and finished tidying the already tidy house, so she went out into the garden to deal with the ravages of the night.

The wind had wreaked havoc—torn flowers off stalks, flung twigs and leaves all over the lawns, ruined young lettuce, broken the stems of sweet peas and runner beans. The garden was a sad sight. She spent part of the morning working out there, staking and pruning and raking up leaves and wrecked plants to put on the compost heap.

When she had finished she went back indoors to wash, flushed, with aching muscles. That was the hardest physical work she had done since she'd left the ballet company and she'd enjoyed it. As always, it had changed her mood; she felt more positive, less weepy. Amazing the chemical changes in you brought about by working your body!

Just as she was going upstairs to shower and change she heard the sound of a car engine slowing, stopping, right outside the garden gate. A door slammed, the gate creaked, there were footsteps on the path. Dylan's heart leapt—it must be Ross, home earlier than he had feared!

She jumped back down the stairs, ran to open the door, ready to fling her arms round him, but it was not Ross standing there. Her entire body jerked in shock, as if she had touched a live wire.

CHAPTER THREE

'MICHAEL!' She was so overjoyed to see him that she flung her arms round him impulsively. People in their world were casually affectionate, although she and Michael had never been very demonstrative. He wasn't that sort of man. There was a deep well of reserve inside him; he guarded his mind and heart from casual eyes and even Dylan had never been entirely sure what he was hiding, only that Michael kept his secrets, even from her.

As their bodies met in close, warm contact she abruptly became aware that this was a man she was holding, not some sexless body she had known most of her adult life.

Shock jabbed into her. She hurriedly began pulling away, but Michael caught her face, framing it between his hands, palms against her flushed cheeks pressing in on the high bones, the smooth, silky skin.

Shaken to her roots, she stared up into his hard grey eyes.

'Missing us already, you are? What did I tell you?' His voice was deep with anger, satisfaction, triumph, or perhaps all three. 'I knew you'd be lost away from us. You made a stupid mistake when you married this guy. You don't belong with someone like him.' He stared deep into her eyes and she helplessly leaned on him, like someone paralysed.

In a wail she protested, 'I love him, Michael!'

'You mean you wanted to go to bed with him! Was

that worth ruining your life for? Why didn't you just spend a couple of weeks having sex with him all day until you were bored with it?'

Was that really how he saw love? Did it mean nothing to him but a drive to sate a passing lust? The idea horrified her. Ross was so much more than just a body she desired; he was the only man she had ever met who really meant anything to her.

'Love isn't just sex, Michael!' she protested. 'That may be all you think about, all you need—but for a woman love means a whole lot more than that. I want to share his life, have his children, be with him all the time.'

His blond head lifted: he flicked a glance past her into the house, raising his brows. 'Oh? So where is he now?'

'At work,' she reluctantly admitted.

'On a Saturday?' Michael's tone was sardonic, his face full of mockery, and her flush deepened.

'There were storms last night; some trees came down—he has to clear a blocked road. He's responsible for a wide area of the forest here; he deals with every aspect of it, from planting to fighting fires. He doesn't do a nine to five office job, you know. His work is far more important than that.'

Michael studied her serious face, his own ironic. 'And how long will Mr Wonderful be working today?'

'How can he tell? It all depends how long it takes to clear the road,' she said absently. She had started to think now that her original shock had died away. 'Michael, what are you doing here? Why didn't you let me know you were coming?'

'I brought your car up here for you.'

'What?' She looked past him in surprise. She hadn't noticed the car until now, although how on earth she could have managed to miss it she had no idea! It was parked right outside, the big, multi-coloured tropical flowers glowing as if they were real in the fitful sunlight! You wouldn't think she could fail to see them, now would you?

'My flower wagon! Oh, thank you, Michael!' She ran down the path and walked round the little car, stroking the bonnet, delighted to have it back again. 'It will make life a lot easier,' she told Michael, who had joined her. 'It's quite a walk to the village, and I can't go further afield unless Ross drives me. The buses take for ever and there's only one a day to Carlisle. So I'd be lost without a car.'

Michael's mouth twisted wryly as he stared at the landscape: the green forest stretching on and on, the road, the grey/blue sky. No houses, no break in the endless trees.

'How are you going to stand it here? It would drive me out of my mind in twenty-four hours. Give me city life any time. You're a city girl, Dylan—what on earth are you going to do with yourself up here? Especially if that husband of yours is out at work all the time!'

It was a question she had been turning over ever since she'd first arrived here and realised for the first time how remote and empty the landscape was. The lack of neighbours, the loneliness, all compounded by the fact that Ross was going to leave her alone for many hours every day.

But she wasn't going to admit all that to Michael. An instinct told her not to betray anything to him that might give him the idea that she was not radiantly happy with Ross.

Turning away, she walked back up to the front door, Michael following her without hurrying. She didn't look

in his direction but she couldn't help noticing the way
he walked—with panther-like grace, flowing movements
that held both elegance and a disturbing hint of threat.
He wasn't that much taller than her, yet his lean, supple
body was held as taut as a stretched wire, making him
seem tall. Why had she never noticed any of that before?
Or had custom hidden his masculinity from her during
their long partnership?

'Oh, I have lots to do every day,' she flung over her
shoulder, glad he couldn't see her face as she spoke;
Michael had always been able to read her expressions.
'The house, the garden...I've discovered a real interest
in gardening.'

'So I see,' he drawled. 'You carry quite a bit of it
around with you, too!'

Dylan darted into the hall and surveyed herself in the
mirror hanging just inside the door. Streaks of mud ran
down one cheek, decorated the tip of her small nose.

She began to laugh. 'Don't I look a sight! You should
have told me! I must have brushed a muddy hand across
my face.' She looked down at her hands, grimacing.
'Yes, that must be it.'

Michael closed the front door and suddenly Dylan became very aware that they were alone in the house. A
frisson ran down her spine, worrying her. How many
times had she been alone with him over the years since
they first met—in his flat or her own, in dressing rooms,
on a bare stage, in rehearsal rooms? She had never been
conscious of being alone with him before. What was the
matter with her?

Had he really changed? In such a short time? She tried
to remember how he had looked last time they met, but
there was a blankness in her memory, as if Michael was

just an outline, a cut-out shape with nothing solid inside it.

Had she simply stopped looking at him years ago? Yes, maybe. And all that time he had been changing, developing... Well, for a start, how long had he been this powerful? They had met when they were scarcely out of their teens. She still remembered him as he had been then, a skinny, slightly built boy with a mass of soft fair hair and light grey eyes. That boy had gone for ever. Now, under his white shirt, she saw the ripple of chest and arm muscles; his shoulders were wider, his blue jeans were moulded to strong thighs and calves. She was looking at a tough, hard-boned, disconcertingly physical man.

Huskily, strangely nervous, she said, 'Phil was going to collect my car.'

'I know. Your sister wrote to me, sending a selection of wedding photos. She mentioned that Phil was going to be coming to London to pick up your car, so I rang her and offered to drive it up here.' Michael wandered away as he spoke, exploring the ground floor of the house, looking into rooms curiously. 'Not exactly stylish decor, is it?'

She couldn't deny it; the house was a square, modern box, built of grey stone, with a slate-tiled roof. Neat enough, but it had been decorated by a previous tenant in a muted style which showed little imagination or invention. The colours of the rooms were safe, pale pastels, the ceilings white, the carpets dull blue or green, the curtains matching them.

Defensive against any criticism he made of her new life, she told him, 'We're going to redecorate when we get time.'

'Time is something you'll have plenty of now, Dylan!'

The sarcasm made her wince. It was painfully undeniable. If there was one thing she had plenty of it was time.

The opposite had been true most of her life—she had lived by clocks, running from bed to rehearsal, to costume fittings, to performance and so back to sleep. Never enough time, never a moment to relax. It had been a terrible strain, one she had begun to yearn to end. She had ached for another way of life—for lazy mornings in bed, a light-hearted drift through the day, long lunches, sunny afternoons on a lounger in a garden, an endless holiday.

Now suddenly she had time and very little to fill it with, and she was appalled at the prospect of life being the same for ever and ever, amen. She found she couldn't sleep late; she had been trained to get up early and she still did so. Long lunches were out because she had nowhere to lunch and nobody to lunch with. Lounging around in the garden soon palled, which was why she had started gardening. She was lonely and hadn't enough to do, but she couldn't admit that to Michael.

She said huskily, 'I expect I'll soon make a start on the house, but I want to settle in first. It was kind of you, but you didn't have to come all this way just to deliver my car. How will you get back? You know you hate travelling by train.'

She hoped he wasn't expecting her to offer him a room for the night. Ross would be furious if he got back to find Michael staying with them. He would welcome any other friend of hers, but never Michael.

His grey eyes held a spark of derision, as if he had read her thoughts and mocked her.

'Trying to get rid of me already, Dylan?'

'No, of course not,' she stammered, very pink.

'Don't worry, I'm dancing on Monday. I have to get back. I've already arranged to hire a car from a national firm with offices in Carlisle. I'm to deliver it back to their nearest London branch.'

'I might have known you'd work out a solution.'

'Yes, you might. I always do work out solutions to my problems.'

The hair stood up on the nape of her neck. What did he mean by that? She didn't like the look in his grey eyes. Michael was tricky and devious. He was planning something—but what? It was something to do with her, that she was sure about.

'Will you drive me to pick up the hire car this afternoon?'

'Of course—Carlisle, did you say?' How could she refuse after he had gone to so much trouble to deliver her car to her.

'Yes. I looked at the map this morning and realised how easy it would be to visit Hadrian's Wall on the way to Carlisle. I'd like to take a look at it *en route*, if that's okay with you? Have you been there yet?'

She shook her head. 'Ross is going to take me when…'

'When he has time,' Michael drily concluded for her, and she flushed.

'Well, he is very busy.' She resented his constant sniping, but she didn't want to have a row with him so she walked away, into the kitchen. 'I'll make some coffee—can I get you something to eat?'

'I had some fruit for breakfast, thanks, at the hotel I

stayed at *en route*. You know I never eat anything more
than that for breakfast. I thought we'd stop for a salad
lunch at a pub somewhere on the road to Carlisle.' He
looked her up and down, his mouth curling. 'Run up and
wash and change—you can't go anywhere in those
muddy jeans! I'll make the coffee while you do that. I'll
soon find out where everything is, and I always did make
better coffee than you.'

She laughed, suddenly light-hearted at the memory.
'Okay, you did. Right. I won't be long.'

In fact, she was relieved to get away for a few
minutes. It would give her a chance to recover her bal-
ance after the shock of seeing him on her doorstep out
of the blue, and her strange, unexpected reactions to being alone with him.

After stripping off her clothes, she stepped under the
shower, hoping that cool water would bring her temperature down. Was the heat of her body due to the hard
work she had done in the garden, or the way being close
to Michael had made her feel?

But how had he made her feel? she asked herself un-
easily. She had never fancied Michael; she didn't fancy
him now. Ross was the man she loved. Wasn't she simply seeing Michael in this new, disturbing fashion because she and her whole world had changed, because
she was not the same woman who had known him,
worked with him every day for years?

During that time she had never really noticed Michael
changing. He was her partner. Her friend. A familiar,
accustomed face, an image imposed by long habit and
time.

His body had been her other self, sexless, moving in
perfect harmony with her, constantly touching, always
to be relied upon. Michael could lift her as if she was

weightless, swirl her round in the air with one hand like a doll, carry her effortlessly across a stage on his shoulder.

Of course she saw him differently now because she was looking at him from a new angle, from outside, like everyone else. Michael was still the same man she had worked with all those years, but she was not a dancer any more. She was a member of the audience now—a woman looking in at his world and dazzled by the glamour, the bright lights, by Michael Carossi's potent image, the charismatic mask of the persona he had developed over the years they'd worked together, the incredible beauty of his body.

Drawing a startled, shaken breath, Dylan stood still under the jets of water, transfixed. How had she been blind to that beauty until now? When they'd been working on that last ballet together, where all they each wore was a body-stocking covering but not concealing them from head to toe, how had she been unaffected? When they'd sensuously twined, body to body, every inch of them in contact, like snakes in a sexual knot?

Eyes tightly shut, she turned the temperature control back to cold and gasped as icy water hit her skin. It was a drastic way to break up those images, but she had to do something to cool down her overheated imagination.

When they were dancing like that, night after night, she had only been aware of the necessity to give the performance every ounce of energy she possessed. Michael had just been her partner. Not a man. Never a man.

She put on a towelling robe and went back to the bedroom to dress again. Michael was wearing jeans; she might as well wear the same.

His were designer jeans; she had recognised the style

immediately; a famous name whose clothes were all beautifully cut. Somewhere she had an identical pair; they had bought them on the same day, from the same shop, at a reduced price in a sale.

Pale and slender in her panties and bra, she rummaged through the clothes in her wardrobe and finally found them, lay down on her bed and pulled them on, wriggling until she could zip them up.

My God! She had already put on weight—not much, a few pounds, but enough to expand her waistline and make her jeans fit too tightly there. She must start exercising and dieting at once.

Pulling on a white shirt, she buttoned it up, slid her feet into white moccasins, brushed her damp brown hair into the usual light curls, sat down and put on some make-up, then hurried down the stairs, smelling the coffee as she descended.

Michael poured it as she went into the kitchen and turned to give her one of his cool, assessing stares.

'Snap!'

She blinked. 'What?'

'We look like twins.' He caught her hand and pulled her over to the mirror in the hall. 'Did you do it deliberately?'

She surveyed their double reflection, finding it curiously satisfying to see them both again, shoulder to shoulder, two bodies which moved as one.

'I didn't stop to think about it. I suppose I put on my jeans because you were wearing your pair,' she admitted. 'I always liked them. They suit us.'

'Yes,' he said, his eyes veiled by half-lowered lids, a slumberous warmth in his voice. 'They suit us.' Did he feel that strange satisfaction in seeing them together? His eyes wandered down over her, then he frowned, staring at her waistline. 'You're putting on weight!'

'I'm not!' she lied, having hoped he wouldn't notice. She might have known he would! Michael was nothing if not observant; he never missed the tiniest detail in production, not just the dancing, but the costumes and sets.

His hands reached for her waist, squeezed hard, making her gasp. 'Oh, yes, you are,' he told her sternly. 'About an inch on your waist, I reckon! That's what happens when you marry out of the ballet. You've been eating and not exercising!'

Guiltily she said, 'It's not a sin to enjoy yourself now and then!'

'Oh, yes, it is, for a dancer! You'll lose muscle tone and be unable to dance professionally if you stop training and put on weight.'

'Michael, I've left the ballet! And I have no intention of coming back!'

His face hardened into a determined mask. 'We'll see about that.'

He was refusing to let her go. She should have known he would. Michael had always been obstinate, set on getting his own way, denying any possibility of failure.

She broke away, flustered. 'Look, if we're going to drive to Hadrian's Wall and then Carlisle, we'd better drink that coffee and get on our way! Are you going to drive back to London today?'

While they drank their black coffee she wrote a quick note for Ross, explaining where she had gone and assuring him she would be back late that afternoon, and placed it where he couldn't fail to see it, in the centre of the kitchen table. He wasn't going to be too happy about it—but maybe she would get back before he did?

As they drove northwards Michael started a tape he had put into the car tape player. 'Like this?'

She listened to the sweet, high pipes with pleasure. 'Very much. It's very unusual. What is it?'

'Music from the Andes. Traditional, played on local pipes, but arranged by a young musician I met in London—he has his own group, formed while they were all at music college. He's part-Peruvian. Solo, he calls himself. His wife and his brother are the other two in the group. I'm setting a ballet to their music.'

'A new ballet?'

'It's going to be exciting, Dylan. Perfect for us—very original, mysterious, haunting...the dance of mountain spirits...all in white, I think...very modern in look...' His voice was passionate. 'I can't do it without you, though. I need you.'

So that was why he had come. 'Michael...I can't,' she said sadly. 'I made my choice when I married Ross. I can't be his wife and a professional dancer. It wouldn't work. You'll have to find someone else to dance with. I told you.'

'One last ballet,' he coaxed. 'Surely he can't refuse to let you dance one last ballet with me.'

'It's not Ross, it's me. I don't want to dance any more.'

'You don't expect me to believe that, do you? You were born to dance. You can't turn your back on it.'

She was silent, listening to the high, lilting music, sensing just how the ballet would look, imagining the two bodies moving across the stage. She knew how Michael's mind worked, the movements he loved, the images he found exciting.

One last ballet...she thought, then thought, No. No. It

was over. All that was the past. She was moving into a future Michael could not even understand.

When they reached Hadrian's Wall it was nearly noon; they visited the sites of several Roman forts, walked around the rough grey stone foundations in the long grass. There were few other people around; there was an eerie silence broken only by the whistle of the wind and the cry of curlews. At one o'clock they had lunch at a pub. The bar was crowded and noisy so they ate in the garden. Michael had poached salmon and salad; she ordered lasagne and salad.

'Not at all bad,' Michael conceded. 'For such a remote place.'

While they ate, they gazed down over a breathtaking landscape. The south-facing views seemed to run on for ever: green fields and grey drystone walls, white stone farmhouses hidden by thorn trees blown into tormented positions by the prevailing winds, a sparrowhawk with pinioned wing and white rump swooping over the hay field beside the pub, the blue sky flowing overhead.

'I have to admit it is beautiful countryside,' Michael said, and she laughed.

'First the food isn't at all bad, now you concede that the countryside is lovely—at this rate you'll be admitting Ross is the right man for me!'

Michael's face froze, grey eyes icy, every bone rigid with rejection of that idea.

'But he isn't, Dylan,' he said fiercely. 'And he never could be. You don't belong with him, or up here. You belong with me, in London, dancing. Turning your back on everything you are and could be is a crime against your own nature. God gave you a great gift and you've deliberately chucked it away. I'll never forgive you—or him.'

She was silent, shaken by his passion. They drank some coffee, not speaking, then drove on to Carlisle where they parted at the offices of the hire car company.

'Good luck with your new ballet,' she said, and Michael gave her a grim, unsmiling stare.

'If you won't dance it, I'll need more than luck. I'll need a miracle. If you change your mind ring me. I shall have to choose a new partner in the next month. God knows who! I want to go into rehearsal with the new ballet some time in the autumn, and the company goes on summer tour to the States in July, remember.'

Her mind washed with memories of other summer tours: humid New York, noisy Chicago, Kansas City, Missouri's wonderful Spanish architecture, long nights of trying to sleep with the wail of police cars and ambulances outside in city streets.

Up early to rehearse on bare stages, the temptations of hot dogs and burgers from street sellers, the buzz of excitement on first nights, the passionate applause of audiences who had never seen them before but who were heartwarmingly generous—it had all been wonderful and exhausting.

Oh, she couldn't deny she would miss it in some ways, but she had done that, been there, got the T-shirt. It was all part of that receding life she was finished with. Sometimes you had to make choices, lose one thing to gain another. Even before she'd met Ross she had known she didn't share Michael's tunnel vision, his utterly focused obsession with ballet. She had loved dancing, loved the friends, the sense of comradeship in the company, loved the applause, too, and even the hard work, but she had tired of the sacrifices you had to make to stay at the top, the difficulty of a private life, the fact that you couldn't have a child because being pregnant meant not dancing for months, meant stretching your muscles out of shape, indeed changed your whole body for ever. After years of it, she had tired of the strains and demands on your energy and attention. Ross had been the catalyst, but she knew she had no longer been so fixated on the life of a dancer before she'd met him.

Impossible to say all that to Michael. He would never understand. Standing on tiptoe, she brushed her mouth against his cheek. 'Goodbye, Michael.' Getting back into the flower wagon, she started the engine, gave him a last wave and drove away without looking back. It was the only way to go.

If she was lucky she would get home before Ross, she thought, as she bombed down the road home. It had been an exhausting day, physically and emotionally. For the first time ever she was happy to see the forest coming into view.

Then her heart sank as she saw Ross's Land Rover parked on the drive in front of their garage. He was home before her. Well, at least he would have read her note and would realise why she had had to go out to drive Michael up to Carlisle.

As she pulled up outside the house the front door opened and Ross strode out, his face thunderous.

'Where the hell have you been all this time? I was worried sick about you. I got back three hours ago. I thought you must have walked to the village so I drove there to look for you, and when everyone said you hadn't been there today I didn't know what to think.'

'Didn't you get my note?'

'What note? I didn't see any note.' He stood beside the flower wagon, staring at it, his frown lifting. 'Oh, I see—Phil brought that ridiculous object, did he? And you just had to take it out at once! Has he gone back already? Why didn't you ask him to stay the night? He'll be exhausted, going straight back home after such a long trip down to London, then up here, and we have a perfectly good couple of spare rooms.'

She was about to tell him that it had been Michael who'd brought her car when the telephone began to shrill.

'That will probably be Alan. He said he'd ring to let me know there were no further problems,' said Ross, hurrying indoors.

Dylan followed more slowly and found him just hanging up. Ross swung to stare angrily at her, eyes cold, mouth bitter.

'That was Phil. He was ringing to check that Michael had delivered your car safely.'

Dry-mouthed, Dylan started to explain, but stammered. 'I w-w-was j-just going to tell you when the phone rang...'

'I bet you were! Just like you left me this mythical note!'

She looked at the kitchen table; it was bare. 'I did leave one.' Bending, she stared at the floor under and around the table, but the note hadn't blown off; there was no sign of it.

'Don't bother with the acting,' Ross bit out. 'I know how good at mime you are! When did he arrive? How long was he here?'

'He got here this morning, but he didn't stay long.'

'You would say that, wouldn't you. Where have you been in your car? Taking him to whatever hotel he's staying at?'

She was torn between a desire to placate him and a resentful desire to shout back. Ross was jumping to all sorts of conclusions before he had given her a chance to explain, defend herself.

She chose to speak softly, not to fight fire with fire. 'He's on his way back to London—I drove him to Carlisle to pick up a hire car. He hates travelling by train; it makes him sick.'

'He got here this morning,' Ross said flatly. 'He didn't stay long. You drove him to Carlisle—you should have been there by lunchtime. So where have you been since then?'

'W-we had lunch at a pub.' Her stammer was back. Her skin was cold and, no doubt, pale.

'And?' Ross was relentless. He wasn't letting her off the hook until he had all the details out of her.

'M-Mi...'' Under Ross's cold eyes she could not get the name out. 'He wanted to see Hadrian's Wall while he was up here. He's always been interested in Roman history; he gets some of his inspiration from history, myth...the past generally. We weren't there long. We just walked around one or two sites, and then I dropped him in Carlisle after lunch.'

Ross took a step closer, staring into her nervous eyes. 'Did anything happen between you?'

Heat ran up under her skin. 'Wh-wh-what?'

'You know what I mean—the man's obsessed with you. Did he try to make love to you?'

'No! Michael doesn't feel that way about me at all. Ross, we were partners and friends—never lovers. I told you that.'

'Yet he went to all this trouble to bring you that stupid vehicle? Drove all those miles up here! You really expect me to believe that? He must have had a pretty strong motive for doing it.'

Her anger flared then. 'Oh, yes! He had a pretty strong

motive all right. He's planning a new ballet and he was trying to persuade me to dance it with him.'

Ross stiffened, his face grim. 'And what did you say to him? Did you say you would?'

'How can you even ask that? When we got married I gave up the ballet and I've no intention of going back— that was what I told Michael, and I meant every word.'

Ross groaned. 'I'm sorry, I can't help being jealous of him. I know how long you and he were close—you told me yourself, once, that it was like a marriage.'

'But without the sex!' she hurriedly told him.

'I know, I believe you, but I find it so hard to believe he never wanted you. You're so lovely.' He pulled her close, held her, his mouth seeking hers, passionate, demanding, possessive. Dylan put her arms round his neck and kissed him back, leaning against him in weary relief.

Ross sighed a few moments later, looking down at her with half-closed, glimmering eyes.

'I'm starving—what's for dinner?'

She giggled. 'You're so romantic!'

'I am! After dinner we'll go straight to bed and make love all night.'

'Promises, promises!' she teased. 'So, how about stir-fry chicken? I bought a fresh organic chicken at a farm near Carlisle. While I slice some of that, could you rush out and pick me some vegetables? Some tomatoes, a carrot, some spring onions, some nice new peas, a couple of new potatoes.'

He squeezed her waist. 'You only love me for my homegrown vegetables!' Dropping a kiss on her nose, he walked over to pick up the garden trug which always stood near the back door.

'It won't take a second. Start chopping the chicken!'

The door banged shut and Dylan sagged down on to a chair for a moment, eyes closed, breathing carefully.

That had been a difficult few minutes. She was very glad to have her flower wagon back—but she wished to God Michael had not brought it himself.

Please God, too, he accepted her decision about the new ballet, and would not be in touch again. Her silence would tell him she wasn't going to change her mind, surely? Once Michael realised that she was not coming back he would find another partner, maybe someone far better than her. Nobody was indispensable. The world was full of brilliant young dancers. Well, not full of them, maybe—but Michael would find someone somewhere.

She couldn't see him again. It was painful to face it— Michael was very special to her; he always would be— but obviously there was no room in her life for both him and Ross.

CHAPTER FOUR

THEY had dinner with Alan and Suzy the following week. Dylan was determined to be friendly, which wasn't difficult as Alan turned out to be very likable. A big, burly, good-humoured man, with thick, bushy brown hair and sleepy eyes, he reminded her of a bear. He even walked like one, lumbering clumsily as if it wasn't natural for him to walk upright.

'I've never seen a ballet,' he told her, staring as if she had two heads. 'But I love dancing.' His grin spread right across his jowly face. 'Pity I'm no good at it!'

'He isn't kidding, either,' his wife chimed in. 'If you dance with him watch your feet. He'll end up dancing on them.' She looked at her watch. 'Time for dinner soon, I think—I'll get it started.'

'Can I help?' Dylan asked, getting out of her chair.

'No need—I can manage. You stay and talk to the men. Keep them off the subject of football or they won't talk of anything else for the rest of the evening.'

Suzy served marvellous food—salmon and asparagus mousse with toast, followed by grilled tuna steaks and new potatoes with a mixture of vegetables, then a pudding of poached slices of fruit—oranges, apples, bananas and pears—in a light syrup with vanilla ice cream.

'I wish I could cook like that!' Dylan sighed, helping Suzy stack the dishes in the dishwasher later.

'So do I,' Suzy said, laughing.

Dylan did a double-take. 'What?'

'I bought it all ready-prepared from a supermarket. All

60

I had to do was grill the tuna and cook the vegetables. The rest was just an assembly job! Life's too short to spend it slaving over a hot stove. Dinner parties should be fun, not work. I like to be with my guests, not in the kitchen.'

'I must remember that. The food was all so delicious, it never occurred to me that you had bought it ready-made. It's a brilliant way of entertaining.' Dylan had been feeling very nervous about the idea of giving dinner parties. Oh, she had often had her friends and colleagues round for a meal in London, but they all knew each other very well and had light-hearted attitudes to entertaining—she would make a huge pot of spaghetti or risotto, or someone would go out for Chinese or Indian food, and they would sit around on the floor, eating and talking, drinking cheap wine. Now she would only be giving small dinner parties to a limited circle of Ross's friends, none of whom she knew well. It was a relief to know that she didn't have to make it an ordeal—Suzy's way of giving a dinner party made it much easier.

They had no sooner rejoined the two men than Alan jumped up, put a tape of dance music on the music stack and grabbed Dylan by the waist.

'Come on, show me how to dance!'

'Poor girl, don't do it to her! You know you've got two left feet!' his wife said, and he threw a grin at her.

'It gives me an excuse to get my arms round her, doesn't it?' Alan pulled Dylan close and began shuffling around the room with her.

'Hey, watch it! That's my wife whose feet you're treading on!' Ross told him, but laughed as he watched. 'You must be the worst-matched pair in the universe! It's like watching a fairy dancing with a giant.'

Alan stood on Dylan's feet again, and she couldn't help giving a yelp of pain.

'Sorry, did I hurt you?' He let go of her and looked guiltily at her tiny feet in their soft leather shoes.

'Not really, you just made me jump!' she quickly reassured him, but was relieved when Alan sat down again.

'I guess I'm just not cut out to be a dancer!'

'You said it,' his wife teased.

As they said goodnight Dylan told Alan and Suzy, 'You must come to us next time—I'll ring Suzy to work out when you're free.'

Driving home, Ross said, 'I'm glad you asked them back—I had a great time tonight, did you?'

'It was a good evening. Suzy cooked us a marvellous meal, and Alan is darling.' A pity Suzy constantly made fun of him, she thought. It must hurt his feelings and he was such a sweet guy. He clearly adored Suzy, too—but Dylan couldn't quite decide how Suzy felt about Alan. She couldn't imagine herself teasing Ross and making fun of him in front of other people. But she could imagine Ross's reaction if she did it. He wouldn't stand for the sort of treatment Suzy dished out to Alan, and Dylan agreed with him. No wife should ever humiliate her husband in front of other people, or nag him—it had been embarrassing to watch it happening.

When Alan and Suzy came to dinner a couple of weeks later Dylan was worried in case something went wrong, but the evening went off well enough, except that there seemed to be even more tension between the other two. Suzy was as scratchy as an old record—she snapped at Alan every now and then—while he seemed edgy and was far quieter than he had been at his own home.

Ross talked to him about their work while the four of

them drank an aperitif, then Dylan went into the kitchen to get the food ready, quite glad to get away from the uneasy atmosphere.

'Can I help?' offered Suzy, but Dylan refused the offer politely.

'Thanks, but I can manage—you stay and talk to the men.'

Dylan served them grilled prawns with a home made mayonnaise to begin with, then cold poached salmon with salad followed by chocolate mousse she had made herself. The work had taken up most of her day, but she had enjoyed doing it.

'That was mouthwatering,' Alan said, eating a second helping of mousse. 'Did you cook it all yourself?'

She nodded, and met Suzy's wry eyes almost apologetically. 'I'm new to cooking so I decided to try and do it all myself.'

But why was she apologising for not having bought the meal ready-made? It had been fun. Some days she went nowhere, did nothing, saw nobody—except Ross for a few minutes in the morning before he went to work and in the evening before she went to bed. Having to plan for the dinner party, do the shopping, prepare the food, had been new and stimulating.

'Well, congratulations, you get a gold star,' Suzy said with a faintly acid smile. 'Aren't you a lucky boy, Ross? She's not only talented and beautiful, she can cook, too. How will you ever keep her?'

Ross's face clouded over, and he was quiet for the rest of the evening. Dylan felt a spurt of dislike for Suzy—why had she said something so spiteful? How had she guessed that Ross wasn't entirely sure about his marriage? Had Ross confided in her?

Dylan knew he wasn't certain their marriage would

work out—he was afraid she would tire of being married, be bored living right up here in the North, far from any town, let alone a city. He had said as much to her, several times, but she resented the very idea of him confiding his feelings to Suzy.

She didn't say anything to him after the party, though. She was tired and a little depressed; the evening had been a let-down. She had wanted to make it a wonderful occasion, but Suzy and Alan's subterranean squabble had made it uneasy, an evening balanced on a knife-edge.

She wished she liked Suzy better, but they didn't have much in common, and Ross's other colleagues all lived further away. She had no opportunity to meet any of their wives, and as there were no close neighbours she very rarely had anyone to talk to except the shopkeepers in the village.

There wasn't that much to do around the house; she could finish her housework in a couple of hours each morning. But she enjoyed working in the garden more and more. A library van visited the area once a week, and Dylan was able to get out books on gardening, learn how to prune and plant, how to plan borders, work out colour schemes.

One morning Michael rang her, making her nerves skip as she recognised his voice. He didn't waste time with polite preliminaries, just asked curtly, ''Changed your mind yet?'

'No, and I won't, Michael. Please, accept it…'

'Never,' he said. 'And I'll never forgive you. You're deliberately throwing your life away—why? All that talent and you're burying it. It's a sin against life.'

The phone slammed down and she jumped, her ear reverberating with the noise.

From around that time she began to feel very off-colour. She couldn't think what was the matter with her. Her symptoms weren't serious enough for her to go to the doctor, and they kept changing. One minute she had backache, the next she felt sick, then she had a headache. After half an hour gardening she suddenly felt dizzy, the world going round and round, and had to go indoors and lie down. All those little grumbling problems she kept to herself, because she didn't want Ross to think she was a hypochondriac. Her health had always been so good. Was it loneliness and boredom that were making her ill?

'Why don't you join a club?' suggested Ross.

'The only one around here is the mothers' club at the village church, and I don't qualify.'

He laughed. 'How about the golf club? I know Suzy's a member. It's only a couple of miles away. Have you ever played golf?'

She shook her head. 'I've never really played any games—dancers are reluctant to risk injuring themselves, and playing games always seems to end in someone pulling a muscle or breaking a leg!'

'I'd never thought of that, but it's true—Alan is always doing himself an injury playing golf or football. He's so clumsy. Suzy's right.'

Dylan frowned. 'Aren't they happy, Ross?'

He looked surprised. 'As far as I know. Oh, Suzy's got a sharp tongue, but she's fond of the old boy.'

'He's no older than you!'

'You know what I mean.'

She wasn't sure she did, but she dropped the subject. Ross seemed to like Suzy. Maybe she was imagining the tension between her and Alan? It was a pity she and

Suzy didn't get on—she could have done with a friend, someone to talk to about how she felt, the problems she had. She couldn't talk to Ross; she was wary of letting him know what she was thinking and feeling.

The trouble was, she badly missed London and her old friends, and most of all, of course, she missed dancing. She did some ballet floor work every day, but it wasn't the same on your own as working in a room full of others doing their exercises. Here, she had no barre to practise at, and no mirror in which to watch her reflection moving, make sure she was moving her body correctly, getting the right angles, making the right shapes.

In early July Ross looked up one Sunday morning and said, 'Seen this?' showing her the entertainments page of the paper he was reading. A large photo of Michael and a girl dominated the print.

'What's the story?' Was it just that Michael had been seen out with that girl or…surely he hadn't got engaged? Dylan averted her eyes from the fried egg and bacon Ross had insisted on cooking for them both. He would be hurt if she didn't eat it.

'He's found another partner,' Ross said with a distinct note of satisfaction in his voice.

'You're kidding?' Dylan leaned forward to stare at the girl and caught the smell of the fried food, felt her gorge rise. Clutching her mouth, she fled from the table into the downstairs cloakroom where she was violently sick.

When she came slowly back to the kitchen, pale and shaky, Ross had cleared the table, thrown her cooked breakfast away, and was loading the dishwasher. Hearing her footsteps, he looked round, his eyes coldly flicking over her.

'That much of a shock, was it?'

She looked blankly at him. 'What?'

'That he's going to be dancing with someone else!'

'Oh, don't be silly,' Dylan said wearily. 'I knew he would. I'm glad he's found someone.'

'Yes, I saw how glad you were!' Ross bit out.

Dylan simply wasn't well enough to argue with him. Wordlessly she took the Sunday paper from the kitchen table and went into the sitting room to lie down and read the story without Ross's cold eyes on her.

Michael had been holding auditions for some weeks, seeing hundreds of girls, and had finally found a partner to take her place: a girl called Sasha Vienzini.

A faint smile curled Dylan's mouth—that was never her real name! But then there had always been a tradition of ballet dancers taking foreign stage names, particularly Russian ones. English names hadn't been considered exotic enough, although these days dancers chose more and more to use their real names, just as the choreographers and directors looked for more reality in the work they did. English ballet no longer felt it needed to apologise for not being Russian. It had struck out on its own and was a powerhouse of new ideas.

Dylan studied the girl's background and previous career, then looked again at the photo and realised she had met her once or twice. Ballet was a small world, both nationally and internationally. Sasha Vienzini had already got something of a name.

While she was staring at the girl's picture Ross came into the room and she looked up uncertainly at him. Was he still in that nasty mood?

'She's a dead ringer for you, isn't she?' he said in sardonic tones. 'If he can't have you, he's obviously decided to have someone who looks like you.'

'He picked her because she's a brilliant dancer,'

Dylan told him. 'I've seen her dance; she's good. Better than good. And I'm sure she'll interpret his choreography as well as I ever did. I hope their partnership is a terrific success.'

'Is that why you were sick when you heard the news?' he asked, and she dropped the newspaper on the floor, angrily aware that she was still very pale and a little shaky.

'I'm just not well today. Nothing to do with Michael getting a new partner.'

'Tomorrow you'd better go and see the doctor, then,' Ross said unsympathetically. 'Alan suggested we play golf today—are you coming along? You can sit in the clubhouse with the other wives who don't play. Give you a chance to talk to them all. We could have lunch there afterwards. That would save you having to cook.'

'I don't feel well enough,' she said. Suzy would be playing with the men, of course. No sitting around drinking cocktails with other women for Suzy! She was not keen on her own sex; she liked male company—preferably not that of her husband.

'I see,' Ross said curtly. 'Maybe I should have lunch there, anyway. Then you won't have to bother to make lunch for me.'

He turned on his heel and was gone before she could answer. She winced at the slam of the front door, but felt too ghastly to care much about Ross's temper. The sickness wore off as the morning advanced. She got up, washed and changed, and began to prepare a salad to eat with cold chicken and rice flecked with peas, sweetcorn and red peppers.

Ross returned at half past twelve and found her mowing the lawn. 'Why didn't you wait for me to do that?' He frowned.

'I've finished now.' She was flushed and perspiring; it was heavy work in hot sunlight.

'I thought you weren't feeling well?'

'It wore off.'

'As soon as I'd gone, I suppose?'

She looked at him with tears in her eyes. 'Oh, stop it, Ross! Why do you keep sniping at me? Are we going to end up like Suzy and Alan?'

His face changed. 'I'm sorry, Dylan.' He put an arm round her and kissed her gently on the mouth. 'I'm still jealous of that ex-partner of yours, I suppose. The last thing I want to do is quarrel with you. Look, I'll make some lunch for us—what would you like?'

'It's ready—just a cold meal. I hope you don't mind but I wanted something very plain.'

'That's fine. Here, let me put the mower away and dump the grass cuttings. You go and lie down. We'll eat in fifteen minutes, okay?'

After that, Dylan was afraid of mentioning Michael at all. How long would it take for Ross to forget his jealousy? She had married him, not Michael, had given up her whole life for him—how could he be jealous?

When he went to work on Monday morning he kissed the top of her head and reminded her, 'You won't forget to go and see the doctor, will you? I'm worried about you. You don't look well.'

She was worried about herself, so she rang the local health centre, which served several villages in the area, and was given an appointment for that evening at five o'clock.

The woman doctor was young, a little harassed, but friendly. She examined Dylan, asked her a few questions, then looked at her with amusement.

'Pretty obvious, isn't it? You're going to have a baby. You must have guessed!'

Dylan blushed. 'I was beginning to wonder, but I've been taking the pill. We didn't want to have a baby yet; we wanted to wait a year or two, get used to being married first.'

'The best laid plans of mice and men,' murmured Dr Easter, laughing.

'Yes,' Dylan agreed, smiling back. 'When I kept feeling sick in the mornings, and missed a second period, obviously I did think... Are you sure, though?'

'I can't be certain until you've had a pregnancy test. Quite simple.' Dr Easter gave her instructions. 'We'll soon know for certain.'

Ross rang to say he would be working late this evening. By the time he got home Dylan was in bed asleep and he didn't wake her; he slept in the spare bedroom and left next morning at first light. She found a note from him on the kitchen table saying he might be a little late again that evening; they were very busy marking trees to be felled and planning a new plantation for the following autumn.

'Give Suzy a ring and meet her for lunch or coffee,' the note ended, but Dylan didn't feel like seeing Suzy. That morning, early, she took her pregnancy test to the doctor's surgery and was given the results later that day.

Smiling, Dr Easter told her, 'You're definitely pregnant. I hope you're happy about that, even though it's such a surprise?'

'I'm not sure,' Dylan confessed frankly. 'I want children, but...oh, I'm feeling so ill, and I'm worried about coping with a baby.'

'You can go to classes here at the health centre to show you how to cope, and the first months are the worst. Once you're over the morning sickness you'll feel better than you've felt for years. Have you told your husband you may be pregnant?'

'Not yet.'

'Do you think he'll be pleased?' The doctor watched her closely, her face sympathetic.

Dylan was flushed and uncertain. 'I don't know. I'm not sure. He didn't want to have children yet, but he wanted them some time…I'm not sure how he'll react to the idea of starting a family so soon.'

'You haven't been married long, have you?'

Dylan shook her head. 'Just a few months. We're still getting used to each other.'

'Well, I'm sure you'll find he'll be very excited. Babies bring their own love with them, you know. If he wanted to start a family some time then he'll quickly get used to the idea that some time is now! You'll get used to the idea too, don't worry. I can see you're a little shaken, and it does take some getting used to—being pregnant causes a lot of changes to the body and in the beginning it can be difficult. The morning sickness will pass off quite soon, and then you'll feel much better.'

Before Dylan left the doctor gave her advice on how to cope with the next few weeks and told her that the baby would arrive the following year, in late January.

'Not the best time of year to have a baby, I'm afraid! Next time I should plan to have the baby in the spring— much easier. Too hot in summer, and too cold in winter.'

'I haven't got used to the idea of one baby, let alone others!' Dylan protested, and as she drove off in the flower wagon tried to absorb the idea that she was pregnant—but it seemed unreal, unbelievable.

She looked down at her body—was there really a baby inside her? She didn't look any different. Stopping at traffic lights which showed red, she put a hand down over her waist and abdomen—she was still slim, but for how much longer? The idea of ballooning was horrible. She had never been fat in her life. She was going to hate it.

She told Ross that evening when he got back, just after nightfall. He came over to kiss her. 'Are you feeling better? Did you go to the doctor?'

She nodded shyly, finding it hard to break the news.

'What did he say?'

She moistened her lips, swallowing. 'Ross...well, Ross...w-we're going to have a baby.'

He wasn't visibly startled or shaken. He merely watched her with unrevealing, intent eyes and said calmly, 'I wondered if that might be it. I talked to my sister on the phone the other day and when I said you'd been sick a couple of times lately and were pale and listless she immediately said you must be pregnant. How do you feel about it, Dylan?'

'I don't know. How do you feel?'

'I'm happy if you are,' was all he said, giving her no real idea what he thought. 'You'll have to take care of yourself from now on; no heavy gardening. Put your feet up in the afternoon and make sure you get plenty of rest.'

He sounded omniscient, but spoilt the effect by adding, 'That's Ella's advice, anyway. But she said you were so fit and had such well-developed muscles you'll have an easy birth.'

'Why didn't you tell me you thought I might be having a baby?' Dylan asked him a little resentfully. He confided in his sister, he confided in Suzy—why didn't he ever confide in her? Looking back over the months since their marriage, she couldn't remember him talking to her as easily as he seemed to talk to either of the other two women. It seemed to her that he kept her at arm's length. Only in their bed were they ever intimate; was passion all he wanted to share with her?

'I didn't want to upset you if it hadn't occurred to you.'

To Dylan's disturbed mind that sounded as if Ross didn't want a baby, at least not yet. If he thought the mere idea of having a baby might upset her he didn't know her very well, for one thing, and, for another, it must have upset him, or why would he be reacting like this?

'Also,' he said, 'Ella could have been wrong. You might not have been pregnant, and then you might have been disappointed—it seemed better not to say anything, and wait and see.'

That had been thoughtful, but Dylan wished he would talk to her, not his sister, and that he wouldn't keep what he was thinking to himself. They were married, for heaven's sake! It was time he started treating her as his wife, not some stranger he merely happened to be sleeping with!

The summer was beginning to wane by the time Dylan had got over the worst of her pregnancy, had stopped being sick and feeling queasy every time she tried to eat.

Ironically, as her health improved the weather worsened. Winds blew rain across the hills; it was damp and cold outside. By evening she often had to light a fire in the sitting room hearth or the house seemed grey and chilly. On the edge of the forest trees turned gold and brown, beech, birch and sycamore began to shed their rustling leaves, which blew across the lawns and lay in heaps, the rain soaking through them until they turned cobwebby, skeletal.

For a few weeks her garden borders were filled with

autumn colours; orange and fire-red dahlias burnt against hedges, and then warm russet and gold chrysanthemums, competing with purple Michaelmas daisies, but at last even these last flickers of summer died away.

The green fern turned brown and withered, the outer barrier of trees grew bare, and the dark interior of the pine forest seemed to Dylan to intensify, come closer. The lower trunks of trees were brown and withered, shut out from the sun because they were so close set; only the upper branches were green. If you walked into the forest a deep layer of pine needles crunched underfoot and dry clouds of dust rose at every step, choking you, unless it had just rained.

She had begun to hate the forest and would never go in there with Ross any more. He didn't argue. Not that she saw much of him, even less than she had during the first months of their marriage.

He was even busier. Autumn was the time of planting, and Ross was out at work from first light until dark most days. She saw very little of him during the week, but if he wasn't working at weekends he came shopping with her, took her out to lunch at Carlisle or one of the little market towns within easy driving distance.

But as the autumn wore on into winter the sunshine grew rarer and the winds fiercer. Dylan discovered what a windy corner of England they lived in. In London she had always been able to ignore the weather, dive in and out of buses or the underground, find plenty to do indoors, go to cinemas, museums, galleries. Up here nature refused to be ignored.

She was kept awake at night by the wind tugging at their roof, roaring over the fields, whistling through the trees, pulling some of them down, damaging roofs and power lines.

She could have borne all that if Ross had been beside her in the bed, but as her body changed, swelling like ripe fruit, dark blue veins appearing on the full breasts which had once been so small and firm, Ross started sleeping in a spare bedroom. He said he didn't want to wake her up in the early mornings when he had to get up to go to work. But he wasn't making love to her any more, and Dylan knew why.

As she was driving home from the antenatal clinic one darkening November afternoon she passed the forest entrance and slowed, noticing Ross's Land Rover parked there.

A second later she recognised the car parked right next to his. It was Suzy's car, but Suzy was not in it. She and Ross were sitting in the back of his vehicle, very close together, their heads almost touching.

Dylan stared, dry-mouthed in shock, then instinctively put her foot on the accelerator and drove past.

When she got home she went indoors, moving like a robot, and made herself a cup of tea. She was shivering from head to foot. It was a chill, wet November day, but that wasn't why she was so cold. She was in shock.

Sitting in front of the living room fire, she clasped the cup between her palms, staring into the flames, seeing it all again, like some slow-running film inside her head.

They had been so absorbed in each other that they hadn't noticed her. Jealousy ached like a knife-wound, agonising, making her feverish and icy cold at one and the same time.

Suzy was beautiful, sophisticated, sexy—and she wasn't pregnant. Dylan knew Ross found her body a turn-off these days. When they'd first met he had watched her all the time, his eyes passionate. Now he rarely looked at her, and when he did he hurriedly looked away again.

Oh, God, she thought, tears in her eyes—what was she going to do? Confront him with it? Accuse him of having an affair with Suzy? But what if he wasn't? What if it hadn't yet developed that far? He would laugh at her, be angry with her—but, even worse, if it had never even occurred to him before she might put the idea into his head! She was certain it had occurred to Suzy, who was very obviously not happy with her own husband. Dylan hated hearing the other woman nag poor Alan, snipe at him, constantly run him down.

A shiver ran down her spine. Did Ross talk about her to Suzy? Did Suzy know they weren't sleeping together, had separate rooms?

She couldn't bear the idea. To stop herself thinking about it she went into the kitchen and made a casserole for dinner. When it was in the oven she went upstairs and had a long, warm bath, then lay down on her bed for an hour.

She was in the kitchen later that evening, checking on the dinner, when Ross got home and came into the house on a flurry of leaves and rough wind, his face flushed, hair ruffled.

'What a miserable day! Winter's really here now. I'm starving,' he told her. 'What's for dinner? Can we have it early?' He joined her and sniffed the air. 'Smells of garlic—what's cooking?'

'Pot au Feu,' she said, her voice sounding unbelievably normal. She didn't know how she was managing to talk, let alone smile, but she did it. 'Beef braised with vegetables for a couple of hours—it can be served whenever you like. Do you want dumplings in it?'

'Yes, please—I'll just wash and change out of my work clothes. Twenty minutes' time?'

How polite he was, talking to her as if to a chance-met stranger! Their marriage had withered like the summer leaves; only the pale skeleton of it remained, and he behaved as if nothing was wrong. Dylan found it hard to believe they had ever been passionate lovers. Did love always wear out this quickly?

He kissed her lightly on the cheek. He smelt of winter, wind, pine; his skin was cool on her own. She had given up everything for him and now she didn't know who she had married—who was he, this stranger she had thought was her husband? What did he really think, feel, want?

'I won't be long,' he promised, smiling at her. The smile of the betrayer, she thought, watching him go out, biting her inner lip. She had never been so unhappy in her life, or so scared.

CHAPTER FIVE

THAT winter was the longest of her life—she began to think it would never end. Just before Christmas Ross told her he had to go away for a night. 'I'm sorry, they sprang it on me out of the blue, but I have to go. This is a vital meeting; I must be there!' Taking a clean shirt from the wardrobe, he began shrugging his broad shoulders into it.

Dylan swallowed, her throat moving convulsively as she watched him with a mixture of anger and helpless desire. Before he buttoned the crisp white linen of the shirt she could see his naked chest, a ruffle of dark hair, the gleam of smooth flesh. He was always vibrant with health, his body lean and fit and agile, and she felt clumsy and ugly.

They had not made love for weeks now and her body ached for him, yet at the same time she sometimes felt she hated him. It was all his fault she couldn't stand to look into a mirror at the moment. The sight of her heavy, swollen body, those full, aching breasts, with their enlarged, dark-circled nipples, made her want to scream, especially when she remembered how she had looked a year ago.

Bitterness thickening her voice, she muttered, 'I don't want to be left alone here all night, Ross! Especially as tomorrow is Christmas Eve! How can you even think of leaving me alone at this time of year, miles from anywhere, with nobody to turn to if anything goes wrong?'

'Nothing is going to go wrong! Why should it? I'll

only be away for one night, for heaven's sake!' He pulled dark brown cords up over his long, dark-haired legs, belted the waist and reached for a green sweater.

He wasn't looking at her, though. He rarely did lately. He hadn't really looked at her since the autumn turned to winter and her body changed so drastically. He couldn't bear to see what was happening to her, any more than she could. Her body turned him off. That was why he rarely touched her any more. Who would fancy a woman who looked like a great pink balloon when she was naked? She fought against tears which were burning under her lids. Ross hated it if she cried. He wanted her to be as strong and down to earth as he was. Sometimes she wondered how it was possible to go on loving someone you knew did not love you.

But she was desperate not to be left alone here. 'Ross, I'm really worried,' she pleaded. 'I don't like the look of the sky and it's so cold, even with the central heating on. I think it's going to snow. If it does, and the phone lines go down the way they did during that last thunderstorm, I wouldn't be able to call anyone for help if...'

'If, if, if!' Ross muttered impatiently. 'For God's sake, stop working yourself up into a state. You're letting your imagination run away with you again. You know what it does to your blood pressure if you get upset. Dr Easter warned you about that. She says you're the creative type, you can't help it, and I'm sure she's right.' His mouth twisted angrily. 'You should have come with a government health warning. Dancing ballet can be bad for your health!'

'What has dancing got to do with it?'

'I know you miss your old life. Don't pretend you don't!'

Honesty made her hesitate. 'Well, now and then, but…'

'Do you ever hear from him?'

She didn't pretend she didn't know who he meant. 'No,' she said flatly, meeting his eyes.

'There was a review of this new ballet in the paper the other day; Suzy showed it to me. It seems to be a big hit. They're going on a world tour with it, it said.'

'Yes, I saw reviews of it.' She had bought a pile of newspapers after the first night and read them avidly, then burnt them in the garden trash burner so that Ross shouldn't know how much Michael and the ballet still mattered to her. 'I'm very glad for them, him and his new partner.'

She saw the flicker of disbelief in his face. 'Are you really? Even though it should have been you? Don't tell me you don't wish you had been the one to create that part?'

'It was my decision, my choice,' she said levelly, knowing she was lying but refusing to admit it. Only a saint would not have envied the new girl the chance to create an entirely new role in such an important ballet, and Dylan was no saint.

'Does that make it any easier to bear?' Ross turned away, looked towards the window, frowning. 'It isn't going to snow today. The forecasts all said no snow until the end of the week. I'll be back tomorrow lunchtime, and the baby isn't due until the end of January.'

Taking a heavy tweed jacket from the wardrobe, he threw her a brief, unwilling glance. He must be able to see how close to tears she was, but he refused to take her worries seriously—what else had she expected? They had so little in common. He didn't understand her and she certainly did not understand him.

They were opposites in every way; they came from different planets. They should never have met, let alone got married. She had had no idea just how far apart they were when she made that fatal decision to marry him and give up her career and her life in London. Did Ross regret having married her?

'If you really loved me you'd take me with you!' she accused, and he swung towards the bed, face grim.

'Stop it! You should know by now that I won't stand for that sort of emotional blackmail. You knew the sort of life you were marrying into; I didn't lie to you. I told you I might sometimes have to leave you alone for hours on end. I told you the house was isolated and we had no close neighbours.'

She couldn't deny it. He had told her all that, warned her that his was not the sort of life she was accustomed to, that she might find it hard and lonely, but she hadn't cared then. She had been head over heels in love. All she had registered was that they would be alone together day after blissful day. It had sounded like heaven to her, then.

'It was spring and I wasn't pregnant!' The changes in her body had been mirrored in her mind; lately her thoughts were as heavy as the way she moved, and the weather certainly did not help. Winter was more depressing than she had ever realised during the years when she'd lived in the city. It was easy to forget bad weather when you didn't have to put up with frequent power cuts, when the streets were brightly lit and you could take a train underground, away from the rain and snow.

He sighed. 'I know, you've had a difficult pregnancy, and Ella told me in her last letter that the last month is the worst of all. She always gets very restless.'

His sister had three children; she should know. Dylan

wished Ella lived somewhere nearby—it would be so reassuring to be able to talk to her every day—but Ella's husband worked for an oil company, which meant he and his wife and children lived abroad. At the moment they were all in Dubai, and wouldn't be home in Britain for another year.

Dylan's own sister, who had children too, lived sixty miles away in the Lake District; they could talk on the phone, but that wasn't the same as sitting down to chat together face to face. You could talk more frankly, take time to get out what was on your mind.

Ross sat down on the side of the bed and took her hand. He was trying to be patient and understanding, but somehow, in her contrary mood, that didn't please her either.

'Dylan, I have to be at that meeting. Try to see it from my point of view. My job is important to me. This is an emergency meeting. If I'm not there they may take decisions I don't agree with and it might be too late to change those decisions later. I can't take you with me. I wish I could, but there won't be any other wives coming.'

Eagerly she said, 'But I could stay in the hotel and...'

'Dylan, I won't have any free time. I wouldn't be able to see you. And if you're honest you know a long drive wouldn't be a good idea. You would get bad cramp and backache; you always do lately, even on short drives.'

Bumping over rough roads to go shopping in the village two miles away was making her feel ill at the moment. In every way her body was letting her down, after years of discipline and obedience. She looked up at Ross, biting her lower lip in frustration, wishing she could deny what he had just said.

He put a hand into his inside jacket pocket. 'Look,

I'll leave my mobile with you—then if anything did happen to the phone lines you could still call for help.' He put the mobile phone on the bedside table and bent towards her. 'Feel better now?'

'I'm not a child, Ross! Stop talking to me in that patronising voice. Being pregnant doesn't make me stupid.'

'You could have fooled me!' Ross pushed a hand impatiently through his thick black hair. 'I can't stand here arguing with you all morning. I'm sorry but I have to go. I must get to York in time for lunch with the others.'

He kissed her, his mouth warm against her cold, averted cheek. Her nostrils quivered, picking up his male scent, his skin freshly showered and shaved, his aftershave the fragrance of pines, arousing memories of those long-ago nights last summer, when they had made love in the forest, on a bed of green fern in the warm, breathing twilight.

It seemed so long ago. At the memory she was on the verge of tears again. They had been so happy in the beginning—where had it all gone, the laughter and passion, the closeness and need?

Ross didn't love her any more. He hadn't even tried to cuddle her for weeks; he always slept in the spare room.

He couldn't bear to share the same bed and she couldn't blame him; she took up so much of it and she wasn't sleeping too well, moving restlessly all night, kicking out in spasm of cramp all the time.

'Aren't you going to say goodbye?' he asked, half teasing now, trying to get a smile out of her. 'What do you want me to bring you from York? You can have three wishes.'

Her head swirled with the muddle of emotions she felt

so often lately—anger and resentment, fear and misery. She turned her head at last, her tangled mop of curly brown hair tossing on the pillow, and looked at him bitterly, blue eyes wide and wet in her flushed face.

'Three wishes? That's easy. I wish I'd never met you; I wish I'd never married you; I wish I wasn't pregnant!'

Stiffening, Ross stared back at her, face hard, eyes leaping with rage, making her shrink away from him. Without another word he turned on his heel, picked up the case he had packed last night and walked out, banging the door of the bedroom shut behind him.

Sobbing, the pent-up tears now streaming down her face, Dylan heard him thudding down the stairs, two at a time. A moment later the front door opened and slammed shut.

Anguish burst out of her. 'Ross!'' she called. 'Please, wait...Ross, I'm sorry, I didn't mean it!' She slid her legs out of the bed and stood up shakily, her body clumsy in the crumpled white cotton nightdress. It was impossible for her to move quickly. By the time she managed to get to the window the engine of his four-wheel drive was starting up.

Dylan struggled to push down the catch but it was stiff; it seemed to take her an age to get the window open. She could see the dark green vehicle right outside, with Ross inside it, although all she could see of him was his profile: a tough outline, hard-edged cheekbones and jawline, framed in windblown black hair.

'Look up, Ross! Look up!' she pleaded as she finally flung the window wide open. Icy wind rushed into the room but she was unaware of it at that instant. She was intent on leaning out, waving. 'I'm sorry, Ross!'

He didn't hear or see her; he did not look up. She heard a roar of acceleration, then the sound of the tyres as he took off along the rough, unmade road. She clung on to the sill, listening to the fading note of his engine somewhere in the distance.

Seconds later he was gone, and she was alone, high on the roof of the world, it seemed to her, surrounded by hills and swirling sky.

The red-roofed, white-walled four-bedroomed house was strong enough to keep out the wind from the hills and distant sea which blew so fiercely much of the time. She rarely went out into the garden now, except to cut some of the vegetables Ross grew—mostly winter cabbage and potatoes at the moment, although in spring and summer she'd had an enormous choice to cook with. She had been amazed by how much better things tasted when you had just picked them in your own garden.

She was shivering violently now, her nightie blowing around her. Closing the window with another struggle, she shut the wind out, put her hot, tear-strained face on the cold glass and stared at the bitterly familiar view.

If only she could see another house, a roof, chimneys, a wisp of white smoke curling up somewhere—any sign of other human presence! She ached to see streets, shops and people, theatres and cafés, buses and noise, not this emptiness, however beautiful, where all she could see was trees.

Trees, trees, nothing but trees under the grey, sagging bolster of a sky.

'I hate you!' she yelled at the tall Norwegian spruce with its green needle-like leaves, the mountain ash planted at the forest edge which could be very pretty in spring, when it bore creamy white sprays of flowers, and still had some of those red berries the birds had mostly eaten, and a little belt of cypress whose silvery blue pyramid shape was pleasing to the eye. Ross said they'd planted other trees at the edge of the pines to soften the impact of all those conifers, but nothing could disguise the darkness and lack of life beneath their towering presence.

This was not a natural wood of deciduous trees. No oak, no ash, no hazel. No, here you saw a commercially planted, regimented forest laid out in straight lines on what had once been high, open moorland, rich with heather and gorse, where the wind blew free and every inch was alive with birds and small animals. They had all gone, driven out by the smothering trees. They could not live in that dense shadow and neither could she. She hated living here.

The small of her back was aching; she pressed her hand into it, groaning. She couldn't bear to stay in bed any more; it made her back worse. She might as well get up.

Looking at the clock on the bedside table, she was surprised to see it was already seven forty-five. She had all day to waste, but she might as well get dressed and start on the housework. It took her twice as long as it used to; she never seemed to catch up. At least work would take her mind off her problems, and she would have even more to do tomorrow. This would be their first Christmas together.

Last Christmas Eve she had been staying with Jenny and her husband Phil and their two children, as she had done every year since Jenny had married. This year Dylan wanted to make Christmas very special for Ross, whose parents were also dead and who had not had a family Christmas for years. She had bought lots of decorations. Their tree was already set up and glittering with fairy lights; the rooms downstairs were swagged in tinsel. She had made a Christmas cake and several puddings; tomorrow she would make mince pies, jelly, trifle, all the traditional food of the season.

She walked into the bathroom, her hand still supporting her back, took off her nightie and dropped it into the woven linen basket, then, avoiding the sight of herself in the mirror, showered, closing her eyes with pleasure under the warm water. Stepping out a few moments later, she towelled herself and put on a robe before going back into the bedroom to get dressed.

Gloomily she surveyed the rack of maternity clothes—she hadn't been able to afford a large range of them, and she hated the sight of them all by now, couldn't wait to wear pretty clothes again, in her proper size. The warm cherry-red of a sweater looked cheerful, though. She took that out, and a thin floaty white shirt to wear under it, plus a pair of maternity jeans with an infinitely expandable waist.

Her feet were freezing; she put on two pairs of socks, and then comfortable slippers.

Housework was not her favourite occupation. Especially now that she found it almost impossible to bend down without discomfort, and couldn't lean across tables to polish them.

Once, she had danced her way through the work, made it part of her daily exercise routine, using the backs of chairs as a barre. Not any more. Just getting through the necessary tasks was exhausting. The idea of ballet was something she simply pushed to the back of her mind.

As she brushed her hair she thought of herself two years ago, light as a feather...what had she been then, a size eight? She was only five foot one and had had a diminutive figure, her breasts small and high, her waist tiny, although her legs were quite long for her height.

She had been slender and supple in her tights and black body as she'd rehearsed the new ballets Michael had choreographed for them. 'Exercises for Lovers' he had called it, and the title described it perfectly. Two people meeting, falling in love, parting in tears, coming together again. She had loved dancing it.

The intensity of concentration, the physical difficulty of some of the moves, had used up all her energy, but it had been the most rewarding time of her life. The discipline of that work had occupied every waking moment, obsessed her.

If only she felt that way now! She had thought being pregnant would be as exciting and wonderful as rehearsing a new ballet. Nobody had warned her what it would really feel like.

How ironic that it had been that ballet which had brought Ross into her life and ended her career for ever, changed her body, her life, in ways she had never anticipated.

Stop thinking about it! she scolded herself, dropping the brush on the dressing table. Only another month and it will all be over. Just hold on to that thought.

Slowly she made her way downstairs and began work in the kitchen, washing up the breakfast things Ross had used, tidying the room before getting out the vacuum cleaner.

At midday, flushed and breathless, with swollen ankles, cramped calves, she sat down in the kitchen to eat some soup. Had she had breakfast? She couldn't remember. Her brain was going too, now!

Once she had been so sure of herself and the future she wanted. She couldn't be certain about anything any more; she didn't recognise herself or Ross. Lifting her feet on to a foot stool, she bent to massage her left calf and at that moment the mobile phone began to ring.

He was ringing to say he was sorry! Eagerly Dylan grabbed for the phone, which she had left on the table. She was so breathless she couldn't say anything for a second, and before she could the caller spoke.

'Hello? It's me, darling—Suzy! I can't hear you very well, Ross, the line keeps breaking up—can you hear me!'

Dylan opened her mouth to explain that it wasn't Ross listening, but the other woman didn't pause long enough to give her a chance.

'Darling, I'm sorry. I'm going to be late. Alan hasn't gone yet and I can't get away without arousing his suspicions!'

Dylan sat there, frozen in shock, holding the phone so tightly that her knuckles went white.

The other woman laughed. Laughed! Dylan's teeth met.

'Can't wait to get to York. It's going to be a wonderful night. Oh…can't talk any more, he's coming back. See you soon, Ross.'

There was the sound of a kiss being blown, then the call ended abruptly.

Dylan didn't move for a long, long time. She couldn't believe what she had just heard; the words swirled around in her head. 'Darling' Suzy had called Ross, in that sultry, intimate voice, and talked about seeing him tonight in York. Hadn't Ross said that Alan wouldn't be at this conference? He was staying on duty so that there was someone covering this area of the forest.

That day, last autumn, when she'd seen Suzy and Ross together in the forest, she had told herself there could be a perfectly innocent reason for their being together, that she was crazy to jump to conclusions. But this time there couldn't be any mistake. She wasn't imagining that phone call or the way Suzy had talked, or what she had said. Suzy hadn't wanted Alan to hear her; she couldn't leave yet in case he guessed what was going on!

Slowly Dylan switched off the mobile phone and laid it down. When did they meet? Where did they meet? Obviously somewhere nearby—Ross hadn't been away since their honeymoon. But he was often out all day and long into the night.

There was only one place where he could have a secret rendezvous—hidden deep among the trees where Ross spent a great deal of his working hours. Her teeth grating, Dylan thought of the small wooden hut where Ross kept many of his tools and instruments; she herself had met Ross there many times in the warmer months, taken him sandwiches and a flask of fresh coffee and stayed to talk for half an hour. Once or twice they had made love there on a low cot bed Ross used on the rare occasions when he had to work all night out in the forest on research projects.

That must be where he met Suzy. How long had it been going on? And how serious was it? Dylan dropped her head into her hands, pressed her palms to her hot, aching eyes. No wonder Ross hadn't touched her for weeks. No wonder he had refused to take her with him. He'd said wives couldn't go. The truth was, he was taking Suzy.

But how could he do that without it getting back to Alan? Was Suzy going to sneak into the hotel and keep out of sight? Would they have room service in their room instead of going down to dinner, and then make love all night? In the morning Ross would rejoin his colleagues and while they were in their final session of discussions Suzy would creep out and drive home to an unsuspecting Alan.

Dylan put a hand to her mouth, bit down on her fingers in a spasm of jealousy, to stop herself screaming. The thought of Ross with another woman was agony. She couldn't bear it.

How could he do this to her? He had left her alone here, frightened and miserable, while he was with that blonde harpy. Poor Alan. He didn't deserve what Suzy was doing to him. He adored his wife, thought she was wonderful. And all the time...

Rage flared inside her. Well, she wasn't putting up with it! She was going, leaving Ross. And she wouldn't be back.

Not giving herself time to calm down, she picked up the mobile phone and dialled her sister's number. Jenny was out, no doubt doing last-minute Christmas shopping with her two little boys, but her answer-machine was switched on, so Dylan left a message on it.

'Jen, I'm coming to stay for Christmas—leaving right away.' she looked at her watch. Amazingly, only half an hour had passed since she'd sunk down here for a rest and a light snack lunch. It seemed an eternity.

Her voice husky, she went on, 'It's one o'clock. I should get to the Lake District by about four. See you then. I'll be alone. Ross isn't coming with me. I'll explain when I get there.'

Jenny had invited them to spend Christmas with her, but Dylan had wanted to spend those special days alone with Ross. The irony struck her forcibly as she slowly plodded back upstairs.

It didn't take her long to pack. She left a note for Ross.

Suzy rang you on your mobile. I know all about it now, Ross. I'm going to Jenny. Don't bother to come after me. We're finished.

She dropped her wedding ring on top of the note. Her marriage was over. Barely a year—and it was over!

She refused to cry. She wasn't breaking down again; he wasn't worth it.

Her car was in the garage; the sight of it both saddened and comforted her. Michael had covered it with such enormous, exquisite flowers in metallic, vivid colours, pink and blue and yellow, with huge green leaves.

People stared when she drove into the village, but the little car was still in very good condition. Ross had offered to buy her a new car but she wouldn't part with her flower wagon for anything. It was her last real link with her old life, with ballet and all her friends. None of them were great letter-writers. At first they had rung her occasionally, but it was months since she had heard from any of them. Michael had sent her a postcard from New York a week ago. He and the company were on the last leg of their tour and he was looking forward to opening there soon. Ross had seen the card on the kitchen table, picked it up and read it, scowling. He was still jealous. He wanted her to forget all about the life she had once led. It was alien to him; he had had no part of it.

'Is he still writing to you?' he had asked her, looking up with laser-bright eyes.

'That's the first I've heard from him in months.'

'How's he getting on with his new partner? She looks pretty sexy.'

'I think Michael's happy with her.' She didn't tell him

that Michael had rung her the morning after the first night of this new ballet. It had been rapturously received, but Michael had not been entirely happy with Sasha's performance.

'She hasn't got your fire or your vulnerability,' he had said, sighing. 'She's a little cold.'

She had been secretly pleased to hear that.

'I still think he's gay,' Ross had said.

She'd shaken her head. Michael was intensely masculine, a very powerful man with incredible muscle power although he was so thin. But she knew why Ross wanted to believe Michael was gay. He found it hard to believe that her relationship with Michael had been platonic; they had been partners, friends, colleagues, never lovers, but Ross did not believe in platonic relationships.

As she set off she looked up uncertainly at the sky. There was definitely snow in those clouds. But with any luck she should reach Jenny's house before the first flake began to fall.

Ruth Nicholls heard the noises just as she was making her lunch. She knew what they meant. 'Oh, no!' she groaned. ''Fred's trying to escape again!'

Cleo gazed at her cynically, green eyes aslant.

'Don't look at me like that! I know what you're thinking! What else can I do with him in this weather? He'd freeze to death outside,' Ruth snapped. 'And stop staring at my chicken. You aren't having any of it.'

The thudding noises grew louder. Ruth went to the kitchen window to stare down the garden. The walls of the shed were visibly shuddering under the onslaught.

Angrily, Ruth marched to the back door. 'I wish I'd never brought him here! He is more trouble than he's worth.'

Cleo agreed; she detested Fred, who kept trying to murder her, not that he had any chance of succeeding. Cleo was far too quick-witted and fast-moving. She could also read minds. Especially Fred's. He had a low-grade mind, cunning yet stupid. Cleo didn't even have to look at him to know what he was thinking. She lived on a much higher plane. She had been a queen in Egypt and she never forgot it.

For a second she considered accompanying Ruth to watch what happened to Fred, but other impulses prevailed. A delicious fragrance wafted to her; she hummed softly to herself as she leapt upwards. By the time Ruth had reached the shed Cleo was on the kitchen table eating the thinly sliced chicken laid out on a plate, delicately separating it from the uneatable heaps of salad.

Why did that woman eat all this green stuff? Very occasionally Cleo ate a morsel or two of grass, for private and personal reasons, but Ruth actually appeared to enjoy mounds of herbiage. It was inexplicable, but then most of Ruth's actions seemed extraordinary to Cleo.

From the end of the garden Ruth's voice rose angrily. 'You brute! You stupid, destructive animal! Look what you've done! It will take me hours to put those shelves back up again.'

Cleo had finished her snack. She lazily turned her elegant head in time to see Ruth hurtling backwards at great speed before she tumbled on to the grass. A streak of grey flashed away up the garden. Cleo yawned in disgust. Fred had won again. When would that woman ever learn?

Oh, well, time to go and take a look at the damage he had done to the inside of the shed. Cleo liked to keep a close eye on everything that happened within her domain.

She stepped out of the open kitchen door then paused, shivering, throwing a glance upwards. Livid, low-sagging clouds massed overhead; there was a strange deadness to the light. Wrinkling her nose, Cleo breathed the icy air.

Yes, no doubt about it. Those strange, cold, white things were coming again. She remembered them from other winters. She liked to watch them falling down, if she was feeling kittenish she might even dance on her hind legs to catch them, taste them on her tongue, but they made it very difficult to get about. You sank down into them and they were wet and cold. Cleo hated her smooth, sleek coat to get wet.

Ruth was getting up, moaning, wincing. Maybe at last she would get rid of Fred? Life around here would be much easier if she did. Not so interesting, perhaps.

The phone in the kitchen began to ring and Ruth limped past to answer it, pushing her tousled brown hair back from her flushed, scratched face. Cleo heard her say, 'Oh, hello, Henry, how are you?'

The local doctor grunted. 'Who cares how I am? I'm only here to look after everybody else. I don't expect tender loving care, or even sympathy from anyone.

Ruth recognised his mood. Poor Henry, he was probably being rushed off his feet at the moment. Cold weather always meant a packed surgery.

Drily, Ruth said, 'Glad you're okay. I'm fine, too.'

'Don't you be sarcastic with me, Ruth!' he growled. 'Can't stop. Just ringing to let you know tonight's village meeting has been cancelled. Lucy Prescott is agitated because she thinks it will snow before nightfall.'

'Well, she does have a point. It's freezing today, and if it snows and there's black ice on the road tonight she'll have a devil of a problem getting back up Slip

Hill. It hasn't got that name for nothing! I don't blame
Lucy for taking precautions, especially as it's Christmas
Eve tomorrow...' Ruth stopped speaking, suddenly noticing her chicken salad no longer contained any
chicken. 'That damned cat!'

'What did you say?' The man at the other end of the
line sounded incredulous. 'Do you mean Lucy?'

Ruth laughed. 'Of course not. Lucy can be difficult,
but I wouldn't call her a cat. No, I just realised that cat
of mine has stolen my lunch. While I was making it Fred
started trying to knock the shed down.'

'Real demolition expert, that goat of yours!'

'I wouldn't mind, but I only locked him in to save
him dying of exposure if the snow came, but the un-
grateful creature refused to stay shut up and began crashing his horns into the wall. I rushed off to deal with him
and while I was gone Cleo ate my chicken and scattered
the salad all over the table. I shall have to get myself
something else.'

'Pets are just a nuisance. I don't know why you keep
them! They give you a lot of work and cost a lot of
money At least Gwen took that stupid pink poodle of
hers when she went.'

Ruth was startled to hear him mention his ex-wife.
For months after Gwen ran off with a golf instructor of
twenty-six her name had not passed Henry's lips. He had
been bitterly humiliated. Fifty years old himself, it must
have been a traumatic shock for him to be deserted for
a man only half his age.

Gwen had only been thirty-eight, but she'd looked
much younger, with bright red hair, although Ruth suspected she kept grey out of it by dying it from time to
time, and she wore far too much make-up. She had the

enamelled look of a doll. Ruth had never liked her. They had had nothing in common.

Gwen cared only about herself: her looks, her clothes, her jewellery, her red sports car. She had never seemed to care much about poor Henry, and she'd positively disliked all his patients, spoke sharply on the phone if you rang up, gave people indifferent nods when they greeted her in the village and never got involved in any of the busy social life everyone else enjoyed.

Ruth had had to ring Henry far too often during her mother's long illness and Gwen had made it unpleasantly clear that she resented Ruth's constant pleas for help. Once she had even accused Ruth of being obsessed with Henry.

'It doesn't bother me, Miss Nicholls, lots of middle-aged spinsters have crushes on their doctor, or their vicar,' she had drawled. 'But you're embarrassing my husband, although he's far too polite and kind-hearted to tell you so.'

Ruth had gone dark red, shaking with rage and shame. 'It isn't me who needs your husband, Mrs Trafford!' she'd furiously ground out. 'It's my mother. She is in great pain today and she needs an emergency injection. But never mind, if Dr Trafford doesn't want to come to see her I'll call another doctor.'

She had hung up and stood there, trembling, muttering words she had not even realised she knew and had certainly never used before. It was a cathartic experience. Afterwards, though, she had felt empty and cold, and she remembered it with self-disgust. It was sickening to lose control like that.

Of course Henry had come as soon as his wife passed on the message. His face had been pale and grimly set. Neither of them had mentioned Gwen, for which Ruth had been deeply grateful, hoping that he had no idea what his wife had said to her. They had gone up to see Ruth's mother, Henry had given her a pain-killing injection, and in short, merciful time she had been peacefully asleep.

Henry had left, saying with a pat on her shoulder, 'Not long now. You know that, don't you? Ring me whenever you need me, Ruth.'

Ruth hadn't pointed out that his wife wouldn't like it. She would have been too embarrassed. Gwen's accusation had hurt her, not least because there was some truth in it. Ruth did need Henry; he was all that kept her sane now, towards the end of her mother's illness. She was always so tired, so sad, and she felt so useless. There was so little she could do except try to make her mother's last weeks more comfortable.

But in another sense Gwen was a million miles from the truth. Ruth was not a fool. She knew she was getting old; old and ugly. Her face was thin and angular, her only asset a pair of wide hazel eyes; she had a skinny, lanky body, short, dull brown hair, showing traces of silvery grey. She was not going to make a fool of herself over any man.

She had no close friends in the village, either, because the last five years of her life had been spent looking after her widowed mother. Ruth had rarely left her alone. Crippled by a stroke shortly after the death of her husband, Mrs Nicholls had needed constant nursing until her death a year ago, and Ruth and Dr Trafford had been thrown together by a mutual desire to make her life bearable.

Ruth owed Henry Trafford a good deal. She had felt very sorry for him when his wife ran away with her young boyfriend; she knew how badly Henry had taken it. He had hidden it as well as he could, but Ruth knew him very well. She had seen the lines of pain and humiliation bitten deep into his skin. He knew everyone was talking about him behind his back; some of them laughed, some pitied him. He hated both reactions. Ruth paid him the compliment of never mentioning the subject. She behaved exactly the same when they met. It was all she could do for him.

The divorce had come through in the summer. If Henry was able to mention Gwen without wincing maybe he was coming to terms with what she had done to him.

'Fish,' he said. 'Fish are the only sensible pets to have. Silent and practically trouble-free, and their food is very cheap.'

Ruth laughed. 'Boring, too! Fish are no fun. And Cleo would eat them if I got some.'

She looked over her shoulder as Cleo began caterwauling outside the closed kitchen door, and saw white flakes whirling past. 'Oh...the snow's started, Henry! I'd better go. Cleo is screaming to come back indoors; she hates getting her fur wet.'

'Get a fish!' he advised again. 'Bye, Ruth.'

Dylan didn't even notice the first flakes of snow. She was too busy crying. Anger had given her adrenalin for the first half-hour after leaving home; as she drove she had muttered furiously to herself. She wanted to kill Ross. She hated him. And that woman. Why couldn't she leave other people's husbands alone? She had a husband of her own. She should think about him for a change. Dylan hated her. Hated Ross.

People she drove past on the narrow country roads leading to the motorway gave her very funny looks. She

knew what she must look like. Talking to herself, a di-
shevelled woman in the last stages of pregnancy. They
probably thought she was crazy.

Maybe she was crazy, leaving Ross. She might hate
him, but she loved him, too. But she couldn't stay,
knowing he was having an affair. Her pride wouldn't let
her.

She began to weep silently, helplessly, as she drove.
Luckily, the motorway was almost empty as she even-
tually joined it and turned south towards the Lake
District, so the tears trickling down her face weren't as
much of a hazard as they might have been if she had
been driving on a crowded road. However, her vision
was distinctly blurred, and for a minute or two she
thought she was imagining the whiteness blowing across
the windscreen of her car.

When she realised it was snowing she brushed a hand
across her wet eyes and switched on her windscreen wip-
ers, but they did little to help; the snow was falling faster
and more thickly every minute. This was a blizzard, not
just average snow, she thought, and by now there was
far more traffic on the road.

The further south they went the more cars and lorries
surrounded her. Warily, she stayed in the slow lane, but
that meant having a lorry in front of her and another
behind.

Her back was aching again, she had a tension headache, and when her car tyres skidded on the snow her
whole body was wrenched with fear. She gripped the
wheel, fought to control the skid, her car sliding sideways, and finally managed to pull out of it, but vehicles
around her hooted angrily, making her nerves worse.

She glared at them in her driving mirror, a sob in her

throat. Stupid idiots! Did they think she'd skidded deliberately?

The incident left her shaking, sweat trickling down her back. She was relieved to see that she was almost at the Penrith exit from the motorway. She had meant to go on to the next exit, but she couldn't stand driving in these conditions.

It was a relief to escape on to quieter country roads. She had visited Jenny half a dozen times, but coming from the south more often, before she'd married Ross. She didn't know this approach, from the Northern Lakes. Jenny lived near Windermere, the most popular part of the country, always busy with tourists, even in winter. The landscape was beautiful, but oddly unfamiliar under a coating of white. Trees took on a tinsel look, glittering with ice, fields were sugared and sparkling when the sun came out, gilding the hills and spires of villages hidden among the folds of fields.

She was trying to follow the road signs for Windermere, but she began to have an uneasy feeling that she had taken a wrong turning somewhere.

Pulling up at the next crossroads, she peered at the road signs pointing in each direction—which way now? She hadn't thought of bringing a map with her. She didn't recognise any of those names, and she couldn't see anyone to ask.

Another car came along from her left and took a turning to the right, then a second car did the same—that must be the main road, surely? Dylan followed them.

The road wound downhill steeply. Her wheels began to spin too fast. She was sliding again, the car skating across the road. Terrified, Dylan hurriedly turned the wheel sharply, only to find herself driving down a nar-

row lane which led off at right angles to the road she
had been on at first. She couldn't slow down or stop.
Her car rushed downwards until it finally crashed into a
high wall.

CHAPTER SIX

DYLAN wasn't actually knocked out, but for a moment or two she didn't move, so shocked that she almost lost consciousness, lying across the steering wheel.

When she sat up at last she realised she was in pain. Her seat belt had held but she had been flung forward so hard that she had seat belt burns across her chest and abdomen, and her forehead and cheek ached where she had hit her face on the steering wheel.

Releasing the seat belt with deep relief, she opened the door to heave her body out and winced as she put her foot down. Oh, no, had she broken her ankle?

Gingerly, she moved the foot again. Yes, it hurt badly. She raised her leg a little, very slowly and carefully, because at this stage of her pregnancy a movement like that was not easy, and peeled back her sock. Bending forward to feel the swollen ankle was even more of a problem. She was so sick of being pregnant! The puffy red flesh was tender, but she decided the ankle wasn't broken, merely sprained. She must have twisted it somehow during the crash.

After pulling up her sock again she put her foot down with a sigh of relief, then slid her other foot out of the car. When she put that one on the ground it didn't hurt at all. Gripping the handle of the car for support, she stood up straight. But was she going to be able to walk?

The car bonnet had crumpled on impact, but luckily the base of the wall was cushioned with a mound of earth, thick grass and gorse, which had taken some of the impact. Her flower wagon wasn't a total write-off.

Where on earth was she? Her gaze travelled around the snowy landscape in search of clues, but all she could see at first was fields and trees veiled by the swirling blizzard. It was still snowing just as hard and showed no sign of stopping.

She glanced back up the lane she had driven down but it was far too steep for her to want to walk back up there, especially as she would have to hop on her one good foot.

What was she going to do?

Ross's mobile phone! Thank heavens she had brought it with her. Leaning back into the car, she hunted for it in her bag. At least she would be able to ring for a taxi. She could only be a few miles away from her sister's house. Her fingers skidded over the keys to tap in the code—but when she tried to ring her sister, meaning to ask Jenny to look up a local taxi firm for her, she got the 'No Service' signal. Frantically she tried again. 'No Service'. She closed her eyes, groaning. Oh, no! Ross was always complaining about that. This could be a blind spot, or the weather might be breaking up the radio waves or something. She didn't quite understand how mobile phones worked; they were a bit of a mystery to her.

She leaned on the car, considering her options. Well, she could get back into the car and wait for another vehicle to come along, but what if no other car went past? She would freeze to death out here.

She could force herself to walk back up to the busier road she had driven along a few minutes ago. The hill looked steeper than ever as she stared up to the top.

Surely there must be a farm or a cottage somewhere

around here? Her desperate eyes hunted over the countryside again and stopped as she saw a gleam of light
across the other side of a field. A house! And somebody
was living there because she saw, too, a faint wisp of
grey smoke curling up from a chimney.

Somehow she was going to have to make it to that
house, and the sooner the better. She was getting colder
every minute. Dropping the phone into her bag, she shut
the car door, locked it, and set off.

It was very hard going with only one good foot. It
was going to be painful, and slow, getting across that
field. She leaned on the stone wall for a second and
suddenly realised there was a tree growing a few feet
ahead. Dylan had no idea what sort of tree it was, except
that as it was leafless at the moment it must be deciduous, but to her delight one of the lower branches had
half broken off, hung loosely downwards from the torn
edge where it joined the trunk.

That would make a very useful walking stick to lean
on. Gripping it firmly, she pulled and the branch came
off in her hand. It was almost as tall as Dylan herself,
thicker than she had expected, and pretty strong.

Leaning on it, she limped to the gate, but had a tussle
to force it open because so much snow had built up
behind it. At last she managed to get through, but closing
the gate was almost as much of a problem. When she
had managed that she leaned there for half a minute,
breathing roughly while she peered through the blizzard.

Were there cows in this field? Under the coverlet of
snow it was impossible to guess if a crop was being
grown in there, or if this was a meadow where animals
grazed, but she couldn't see any animals, so she started
off again. She was halfway across the field when she
found herself sinking into a snowdrift.

Close to tears, she leaned on her stick and tried shouting. 'Help! Hello? Hello, can you hear me?'

The wind took her voice away; nobody answered at first, and then suddenly something moved a few feet from her. Dylan gave a startled cry.

What was that? A cow?. No, too small. A sheep? Could be. The shape moved again, came closer. She saw small bright eyes staring back at her. And horns.

Horns? Did sheep have horns? She kept very still, waiting to see if this creature was dangerous. In her condition she couldn't run away. A second later she realised what it was—a goat! Wearing a leather collar and trailing a long chain. Obviously it had been tethered somewhere, but had escaped.

Dylan knew nothing about goats. Warily, she tried to assess this one—was it likely to attack her?

The animal bleated at her, curling back a long, mobile lip. The yellow-blue eyes were a little alarming, there was a wildness in them which worried her, but she risked patting it. The goat bleated again and leaned against her legs. Having company, even that of a mad-looking goat, was better than being alone in this wilderness of snow.

'Hello, goat,' she said chattily. 'Are you as cold as I am?'

The goat stared up at her. She had the distinct impression it was looking at her bump.

'Yes, I'm going to have a baby,' she told it, feeling feverish. It was beginning to get dark now; night would soon fall. She had to find help soon; she would die of exposure if she didn't.

The goat must come from that house over there. Turning the animal back in the direction from which it had appeared, Dylan leaned on it, taking hold of the thick, curly coat which, despite the covering of snow, was warm to touch.

'Nice goat,' she flattered. 'Lovely goat. Come on, show me the way to your home.'

The goat began to move and she clung on to it, but the pace it set made her sprained ankle hurt more. 'Don't trot so fast. I can't keep up!' she gasped, as if it could understand every word she said. She didn't care if she was being ridiculous. She was too terrified that she might give birth out here in this snowy field with only a goat for a midwife.

Ruth had been doing housework for two hours, and was dying for a cup of tea. As she stood at the kitchen sink filling the kettle she gazed gloomily at the blizzard still raging. She had meant to do last-minute shopping tomorrow—the local shops would be shut for three days over Christmas. Of course you might find some of them open in tourist spots like Windermere, but that was quite a drive from here, and parking was difficult there even in winter. She would have preferred to make sure she had everything she needed without having to make any emergency dashes to hunt for things she had forgotten, but this snow was going to make life difficult, if not impossible. Even if it stopped later, temperatures would probably fall after dark; then they would get ice, turning the roads into skating rinks. Ruth didn't fancy the idea of driving into the village tomorrow now.

Just as she was turning to put her kettle on the hob she saw something looming through the blur of whiteness which was the world outside.

Leaning forward, Ruth peered incredulously. Someone was in the field. Someone of extraordinary shape, apparently as wide as it was high. A sort of walking blob. A white walking blob.

And what on earth was its companion? Half the size, just as white, but with what looked amazingly like horns on its head.

A primeval shiver ran down her back.

The blizzard lessened slightly a second later and she got a clearer view. The first shape she identified was Fred. A Fred made much larger and rounder by his outer coating of snow.

How stupid to be scared of Fred! That would teach her to let her imagination run away with her! But who was that with him? As the two of them came through the gate into her garden Ruth stared fixedly, trying to identify the other shape plodding slowly along, holding on to Fred's coat. Was it…could it be…a woman under all that snow? A very fat woman.

'Oh, my stars!' Ruth exclaimed, almost dropping the kettle. Not fat, she realised—just very pregnant.

Putting her kettle on the hob, she hurried out of the back door. The plodding figure raised her head and Ruth felt a pang of pity as she saw the pallor of the small, delicate face. Why, she was just a child! The weariness in the big blue eyes, the tremor of the soft pink mouth, which showed no trace of lipstick, made her look about fifteen.

'Are you okay?' she asked the girl, knowing it for a stupid question the second she'd asked it. Of course she wasn't okay! She was obviously limping, she had cuts and bruises on her face, and she looked exhausted and in pain.

'Sorry to be a nuisance,' the girl whispered. 'Could you ring for a taxi for me…? And I ought to tell a garage. I crashed my car over there...' She waved a hand vaguely at the field.

So that was it! Ruth said comfortingly, 'Let's get you indoors first. You look as if you're chilled to the bone.'

Putting an arm around her, Ruth helped her the rest of the way to the back door. Fred followed, but Ruth firmly shut him out.

'Wait there. I'll sort you out later!'

He gave her a furious glare and stood there, pawing the snowy ground as if about to charge the door. She wouldn't put it past him.

'Don't you dare!' she yelled at him, before turning to look at her guest.

First things first. She couldn't let the girl sit about in those damp clothes; she would catch pneumonia.

'Let me take your coat and boots, then you can sit in front of the range. It's been alight all day. These old ranges burn anything, you know. Such a blessing. I feed half my household garbage into it. I do have an electric hob, too, which is useful if you're in a hurry, but you can't sit in front of that and toast your feet the way you can with a range. What's your name, by the way? I'm Ruth Nicholls.'

As she talked she unbuttoned the girl's snow-encrusted coat and slid it off her shoulders. Her mind was working fast at the same time. She must ring Henry and get him to come out.

'Dylan. I'm Dylan Jefferson.'

'That's an unusual name—Dylan,' Ruth said, hanging the coat in her hallway to drip on to the tiled floor. 'I thought it was a man's name. Welsh, isn't it?'

'Yes, Welsh. It means up from the sea...' Dylan couldn't stop shivering. 'My mother was Welsh.'

Poor girl, she looked as if she was about to give birth

any minute, and Ruth did not want her doing it here. She wouldn't have a clue how to help. The very prospect raised goosebumps on her skin.

'And there's that poet…'

'Dylan Thomas. Yes, that's why she chose that name. She was hoping for a boy, but I arrived, and she had been thinking of me as Dylan, so she decided to keep the name.'

Pushing the girl down on to a chair right in front of the range, and kneeling down beside her, Ruth began to take off her shoes and socks. Imagine coming out on a day like this without boots!

'Oh…' she muttered in dismay, as the second sock came off and she saw the sprained ankle, the flesh swollen and very tender, an angry red. 'Oh, dear, this looks painful—did you do this in the crash? You don't have any other injuries, do you?'

'Nothing serious,' the girl said, leaning towards the heat of the range.

Ruth could see some of them: mostly cuts and bruises on face, hands, neck, which she had noticed when she first saw the girl. It could have been worse. Dylan had been lucky.

'I'll ring my doctor and get him to come out and take a look at you.' Henry would find a bed for the girl in the maternity hospital. At this time of year there were surely not many local women having babies!

The kettle was boiling, filling the kitchen with steam. 'I'll get you a cup of tea. Now, don't put your feet too near the grate; you don't want chilblains.'

Ruth busied herself making tea, covered the pot with her old knitted cosy and got out two large bright yellow mugs. But before she poured the tea she decided to ring

Henry. That was when she discovered that there was no dialling tone.

Her heart sank. She put the phone back, tried again. Still nothing. The phone was as dead as a doornail.

Dylan was watching her anxiously. 'Are the lines down? That was what I was afraid of this morning. Snow always brings the phone lines down where I live.'

Ruth forced a smile, trying to sound reassuring. 'We do have a problem with it here, too. They'll soon have the break mended; they always do. Let's have a cup of tea then I'll try again.'

If she couldn't ring Henry she would have to put this girl into her car and take her to the village. Ruth's home was right on the outer edge of Stonelee, at least a twenty-minute drive to Henry's house, with a sharp drop downward followed by a steep hill rising to the village. Not an easy drive in any weather, it would certainly be difficult, if not downright dangerous, with a blizzard raging.

'Would you like something to eat?'

'I'm not hungry.' The girl folded her hands around the mug of tea and sipped, eyes closed. Ruth had put three spoonfuls of sugar in; if anyone had ever needed blood sugar it was this girl.

'Have a slice of toast,' Ruth coaxed. 'You aren't in any pain, are you?'

Dylan laughed huskily. 'Don't encourage me to be a hypochondriac! I've had little aches and pains every day for weeks; I think my body is allergic to pregnancy. I never even had a headache when I was dancing.'

Ruth looked surprised. 'You were a dancer? What sort of dancing?'

'Ballet.' Dylan sipped her hot tea gratefully.

Eyes brightening, Ruth said, 'I used to love going to the ballet when I lived in London, but I haven't been

for years now. I had to move back up here to look after
my mother, after my father died. She had a stroke, which
meant giving up my job, of course, and my flat in
London.' She stopped dead, wondering why she was
telling this stranger so much about herself. She rarely
talked to anyone about her personal life. This girl didn't
want to hear her life story!

'And you miss it,' Dylan breathed with eager sympathy. 'I know just how you feel—I'm a Londoner, I
only moved up here in the spring, and I still haven't got
used to living miles from anywhere. I miss dancing, and
all my friends and the audiences, and... But it's city life
I miss the most. There's always something to do, theatres, cafés, and you're surrounded by all those other people. You can jump on a bus or a tube train and go across
town in no time.'

'Yes, that's the joy of London.' Ruth smiled at her.
'Do you live near here?'

'No, we live close to the borders, just below Hadrian's
Wall. I was on my way to visit my sister; she lives a
few miles from here.'

That reminded her. She glanced at the phone on the
wall. 'I wish I could ring her to let her know what's
happened—she'll be worried. I wonder if it has been
reconnected yet?'

'I'll try again.' Ruth got up and lifted the phone.
Dylan read her expression and sighed.

'Still dead? Have you got any neighbours with a
phone?'

Regretfully, Ruth told her, 'There isn't a house within
half a mile, I'm afraid. My nearest neighbours are a
builder and his wife, the Horrockses, and they're away
in Canada, visiting their daughter and her new baby. I
do have a car, but I don't think it would be very safe to

try to drive to the village just yet. If we wait an hour or so the snow might have stopped or the line may be reconnected.' Ruth paused, nervously eying Dylan. 'You aren't about to have the baby, are you? You aren't having pains?'

'No, I don't think so, thank heavens.' Dylan smiled at her, picking up her anxiety. 'I'm sorry for putting you to all this trouble, but you won't have to cope with childbirth too, don't worry.'

'Are you worried about letting your husband know you're safe?'

'No,' Dylan said curtly, her face clouding over at once, and Ruth wondered what was making her look so angry and sad. She couldn't ask, of course. They would probably never meet again after today, and this girl would not want to talk about her most intimate secrets with a total stranger. Ruth knew she wouldn't.

'What job does he do?'

'He's a forester—our house is on the edge of his forest. All I ever see is trees now—pine trees mostly; it's a commercial forest. There isn't another house in sight.' Her voice had a bitter ring to it. 'I hate them! But he isn't there at the moment; he's at a meeting in York today.' Falling silent, she stared into the red fire behind the grate of the range, then exclaimed, 'The mobile! I'd forgotten it!'

'Mobile?' Ruth was bewildered for a second.

'Phone. It's in my bag.' Dylan looked around for her bag, struggling to get up.

'Stay where you are. I'll get it.' Ruth had put the bag down on the table. She handed it to Dylan, who hurriedly unzipped it, pulled out the mobile phone and tapped in Ross's code.

'No Service'.

'Stupid, useless thing!' muttered Dylan, trying again with the same result. 'The whole point of having one of them is to use in an emergency, but so far I haven't been able to use this one at all.'

'Is it broken?'

'No, it just isn't picking up the satellite, I think. I'm not sure why. Ross says it depends on the location and the weather. Don't they use radio waves? I suppose the snow is blocking the frequency, or something. I'm not very technically minded.'

'Neither am I.' Ruth considered the situation. 'Look, why don't you have a nice warm bath? I can lend you a nightie, dressing gown and slippers to wear, and I have a spare bedroom you can use. After your bath you can have a little snack—an omelette or scrambled egg on toast, if that's all you really want, or some soup. But you can share my meal, if you like—I think I'll make myself some spaghetti; it's perfect for cold weather, quick and easy and very filling. I've got plenty of to- matoes, peppers and bacon for the sauce. Do you like spaghetti?'

'I love it,' Dylan said, getting up with care. 'And I would love to have a bath, thank you. It would make me feel more human.'

Ross had unpacked his overnight bag and hung his clean shirts in the wardrobe, set out his shaving kit, toothbrush and toothpaste in the bathroom, all at his usual method- ical pace. He liked a tidy space around him.

Looking at his watch, he saw he had fifteen minutes to kill before going down for a drink with his friends before lunch, so he sat down at the small table by the window to go over some notes he had made on subjects he wanted to raise during the discussions later. There was no time to waste. He must make sure his points were hammered home. But it was hard to concentrate, which was usual for him. His mind had always been very much under his control, as fit and disciplined as his body. Lately, though, he couldn't be quite so certain of either.

The bitter row with Dylan was nagging away at him. It had been madness to marry her. They were too different. If only he hadn't been so obsessed with her! He should have known she would never put up with his lifestyle. It was the opposite of everything she had known. She had always lived in a city. She didn't understand country life. She liked crowds. They didn't have any neighbours, and the few they did have had nothing in common with her.

He had hoped she would make friends with Suzy, but before long he had realised that was not on the cards. They were chalk and cheese, opposites of each other. It was a pity. He wished Dylan was more like Suzy in some ways—a little more down to earth, less volatile, less hypersensitive.

Desire had blinded him to everything in Dylan that made her the wrong wife for him. Her beautiful, supple body made his blood run hot, his hunger rise. He hadn't cared in the beginning that she had never done any housework, knew nothing about gardening, was afraid of the forest he loved with a silent, intense passion. All he'd cared about at first was that he needed her, had to have her in his bed every night, the smooth-skinned warmth of her body moulded to his own.

Now he never touched her, slept in another bedroom as much as possible, tried never to look at her. Their marriage, in the physical sense, did not exist any more.

With a smothered groan he looked at his watch. Why wasn't Suzy here yet? She was supposed to slip up to his room in secret before lunch. Nobody must see her. Surely she wasn't going to be late, today of all days?

Turning to stare out of the window, he saw a flurry of white flakes go past and stiffened. Snow! So the forecast had been wrong, and Dylan right. She would be frantic. He had better check that she was okay, reassure her.

Picking up the phone, he dialled hurriedly, but there was no reply. The phone rang and rang. Surely she couldn't be outside in this weather? Remembering that he had left his mobile with her, he tried the number only to be told the phone was not in service.

For several minutes Ross sat staring out at the snowfall, which was clearly becoming a blizzard, his expression grim. Dylan was alone, with no phone.

She would be petrified, and with so short a time to go before the birth she might panic herself into starting labour. He couldn't risk it. He would never forgive himself if she lost this baby. It would probably mean the end of their marriage.

He had to get back to her, make sure nothing was really wrong. Even though that meant letting Suzy down. It couldn't be helped. What else could he do?

The phone next to him rang, making him start. It could be Dylan! He picked it up, said huskily, 'Hello?'

'Ross, darling!' said a warm, sensual voice.

'Suzy, where are you? Downstairs? Come on up. You know nobody must see you.'

'No, no, I'm only just leaving. Alan hung around for ages before he went; I could have throttled him—but I'm on my way now, and I'll see you at around three, okay? Leave the key of the room at the desk; it should be safe enough—everyone should be in this meeting of yours. Bye, love.'

'Suzy, listen, I have a problem—' Ross began, but the line had gone dead.

Damn! He replaced the phone with a growl of impatience. Oh, well, he would have to leave her a note, explaining why he wouldn't be there tonight. He had to let her down. All he could do was hope she wouldn't be too disappointed.

Lying back in the scented warmth of the bath, Dylan idly contemplated her naked pink toes at the far end and suddenly remembered Ross nibbling them one night when they'd shared a bath, each at opposite ends. While he softly licked and chewed her toes he had been caressing her intimately with his own, making her giggle and shiver with arousal.

'I want you,' Ross had said abruptly, in a voice deep with passion, and slithered like a snake up her body, pushing his hands under her weak, wet limbs to lift her, open her, so that he could slide inside, his face pillowed on her breasts as he made love to her.

They had made love everywhere in those early months of marriage. Now they never made love at all.

Was it Suzy? How long had this affair gone on? No, she wouldn't think about it. It hurt too much.

Stifling a groan, Dylan climbed out, dripping, and put on the white towelling robe Ruth had given her, then sat down on the cork-topped bathroom stool to dry herself carefully. Her bruised ankle felt a little better, although the swelling was all the colours of the rainbow now.

Ruth had also lent her a Victorian-style white cotton nightdress, the bodice busy with lace and white silk ribbons, a blue velvet dressing gown which zipped up the front, and a pair of matching slippers. Dylan eyed them uncertainly. Would she be able to get into them?

To her relief, though, they were very loose and capacious and she had no problem.

As she came down the stairs the smell of food hit her and she realised with surprise that she was hungry. Earlier she had felt she never wanted to eat again—but it was hours since her last meal.

Odd how the body went on working even when you felt your heart was dead.

Ruth looked round, smiling. 'How do you feel now?'

'Warm and relaxed,' Dylan admitted. 'The spaghetti sauce smells good.'

'It just occurred to me...I put garlic in, can you eat it?'

'Love it. Is there anything I can do to help?'

'Thanks, but no need. Everything is ready. Sit down and pour us both a glass of wine. Unless you don't drink at the moment? Can pregnant women drink wine?'

'Just watch me,' Dylan said, filling both the glasses on the table.

Ruth came towards her with a heaped dish of spaghetti, topped with the rich, red sauce. As she laid it in the centre of the table the doorbell rang loudly.

Dylan jumped, her eyes opening wide.

'Who on earth can that be? Help yourself, Dylan, while I just go to the door.' Ruth hurried off. Dylan heard her exclaim, heard a male voice reply.

Instantly she thought—Ross! She pushed back her chair, then knew she was crazy. It couldn't be Ross. He had no idea where she was; he was in York with his lover. He wouldn't even be thinking about her, let alone coming to find her. Images rose up in her head...Ross with another woman, Ross making love to Suzy, his dark hair mingling with her blonde strands.

Jealousy and hatred choked her. How could she eat when she felt so sick?

The door into the hall opened and Ruth was back with a middle-aged man. Dylan looked at him, blue eyes dark with pain, and met a penetrating gaze.

'This is Dr Trafford,' Ruth told her. 'By pure luck he happened to be called out to a farm near here and…'

'I saw your car and your footprints going across the field,' Henry Trafford told Dylan, undoing his thick tweed overcoat, which Ruth took from him.

'He loves detective stories,' said Ruth, laughing. 'So he—'

'Used my eyes and my brain,' Henry interrupted, 'and worked out that whoever had been in the crash was here, with Ruth. Doctors and detectives have a lot in common, you know—we both have to use guesswork to form a diagnosis. I guessed whoever had been in the car when it crashed might be injured, so I came to see if I could help.'

Dylan shook her head. 'I wasn't really hurt—just some cuts and bruises, and a sprained ankle, although I have no idea how I did that. But I'd be very grateful if you could ring a taxi firm for me, or drive me to the nearest taxi office.'

Henry made a wry face. 'My dear girl, no taxi could get up here tonight. The hills are far too steep, everywhere is snowed in and the police are advising people to stay put except in real emergencies. I had the devil of a job getting to the farm, and I've got chains on my four-wheel drive. The phone lines are down, too, I'm afraid, and my mobile isn't working.'

Her face falling, Dylan sighed. ''Oh, dear.'

Looking at the food on the table, Henry said, 'You

were just going to eat? Don't let it get cold. It looks and smells delicious.'

Ruth smiled at him. 'Wash your hands and face and sit down, Henry—there's far too much for two.'

'I was hoping you'd ask!' With alacrity he went to the sink while Ruth piled spaghetti and sauce on Dylan's plate, offered her a dish of grated cheese, then held out a woven basket heaped with sliced home-made bread.

Henry sat down, his face pink from cold and wind, running a hand through his curly white hair, and Ruth served him before taking what was left in the dish for herself.

'I'll take a look at you later,' he told Dylan. 'Then I'll have to go—this is the sort of night when medical emergencies pile up. I must get back to my surgery in case I get called out again.'

'I hope your patient is okay now,' Dylan said shyly.

'My patient?' he repeated, looking puzzled.

'At the farm?'

His face darkened, and he said curtly, 'No, he died, I'm afraid.'

Ruth looked at him in concern. 'Oh, I'm very sorry, Henry. We'll miss him.'

Dylan wished she hadn't asked, but Henry shrugged his broad shoulders.

'Oh, he was in his eighties and had been very ill for a long time. It was a blessed release for him, and for his family. Can I have some more bread, please, Ruth?'

Dylan watched Ruth cutting bread, giving him two slices, saw their eyes meet and a smile flash between the two of them. Obviously they were very close—just good friends, like her and Michael, or something more than that? She didn't know them well enough to guess.

'More wine?' Ruth asked, and he sighed.

'Wish I could, but I can't afford to drink too much tonight. I need all my reflexes working perfectly.'

Dylan found him an uneasy companion; his combination of hard common sense and offhand courtesy had a bitter tang to it. She sensed he did not like women much. There was a coldness in his eyes whenever he looked at her, amounting almost to rejection, and it hurt. She was in a state to find any rejection, even that of a stranger, painful to take.

Suddenly he said, 'What the hell's that?' staring at the glass door out of the kitchen into the garden.

Ruth and Dylan looked round and both laughed.

'It's only Fred,' Ruth said. 'I must go and put him in the shed when I've finished eating. He must be freezing out there, but he almost knocked the shed down a few hours ago. He hates being locked in there. What he wants is to get in here, but he would cause havoc'

Pushing away his empty plate, Henry gave a satisfied sigh. 'That was terrific, Ruth. You're a good cook. You should open a restaurant; I'd be one of your best customers.'

'Too much like hard work,' Ruth said.

He laughed. 'Well, if you've finished eating, Dylan, I'll check you out before I have to go. Ruth, will you be our chaperon?'

The examination was brief but thorough; he looked at her bruises, listened to her pulse, took her temperature, then listened to the baby's heartbeat through his stethoscope, inspected her ankle and agreed with her own diagnosis.

'You'll do, but I think you should stay here tonight—it would be unwise to try to travel in these conditions. By morning the phones should be working okay.' He looked at his watch. 'Sorry, must dash. Thanks for the meal, Ruth, best I've had for ages.'

Dylan caught sight of Ruth's face, saw something in the twist of her mouth, her hazel eyes, that made Dylan wonder. Maybe this was not such a platonic relationship after all, at least where Ruth was concerned. Or was she imagining things?

Ross was just leaving his hotel when the receptionist called him back. 'Mr Jefferson, an urgent phone call for you!'

It must be Dylan, he immediately worked out, hurrying back, but the voice was that of her sister, Jenny, sounding upset.

'Ross? Oh, thank goodness. I remembered Dylan told me you were going to some meeting in York but I wasn't sure which hotel she had said you would be staying at. This is the third one I've tried! Ross, Dylan hasn't arrived yet. There's a blizzard raging outside, and I'm worried about her.'

CHAPTER SEVEN

ROSS sat in the hotel reception, thinking hard for several minutes, then he rang the police station in the village close to his home.

'Hi, John, Ross here—have you been past my house today? I'm worried about Dylan. She isn't answering the phone, but she was supposed to be staying with her sister tonight and hasn't arrived. I wondered if you'd seen lights in our house?'

The local constable had a slow, calm way of talking. He took his time replying. 'No, there weren't any when I drove by at five o'clock, although everyone else had their lights on indoors—it was pretty dark by then. So, as you'd asked me to keep my eye on the place while you were away, I thought I'd better check Dylan was okay. I rang the doorbell, but nobody came, so I took a walk around, looking in the windows—no sign of anybody inside, and I noticed that the flower wagon wasn't in the garage, so she must be driving. If she hasn't reached her sister's soon I should get on to the police down there.'

'Thanks, John, I will. Look, this is the sister's phone number. If you hear anything, you can reach me there.'

He put down the phone and walked out of the hotel, anxiety churning in his stomach. What had happened to Dylan? Where was she? If her car had gone she must have set off for Jenny's—why hadn't she arrived yet? Horrific images filled his head as he started the engine and slowly drove out of the hotel car park. God, what had possessed her to leave home in this weather?

It took him what seemed an eternity to drive from York to the Lake District, heading for Jenny's house; there was no motorway between the two parts of the country—he had to use the ordinary roads, which were icy and dangerous, so that it wasn't safe to drive at anything but a snail's pace. It was very late when he arrived, but Jenny and her husband were still up. There were lights all over the ground floor of the house, and Christmas lights flashed on and off on the Christmas tree in the window of the sitting room.

When he rang the bell the front door burst open within seconds. Jenny, in a hyacinth-colour woollen dress, stared at him in disappointment, looking past him, obviously hoping to see her sister behind him or in his car.

'She isn't with me,' Ross said flatly, his own heart sinking. 'She hasn't got here, then?'

Tears welled up in Jenny's eyes. She had her sister's colouring, but in a brighter shade; her brown hair had a tinge of red, her eyes were bright sapphire-blue, her skin was matt white and she had a warm, rounded, matronly figure which had always been fuller than her sister's slight, slender body. Five years older than Dylan, she had looked after her little sister like a second mother and they remained very close.

'No. Oh, Ross, I'm getting really worried. I rang the local police, but they had no reports of her being involved in an accident, or taken to hospital around here.'

He followed her into the house and nodded to Jenny's husband, Phil. 'Sorry to arrive at this hour...'

Phil made a reassuring gesture. 'My dear chap! We're as worried as you are. Glad to see you.'

Ross smiled gratefully at him. 'I talked to our police

back home; she isn't there. Her car had gone, so she certainly left—something must have happened to her.' His voice deepened, roughened as he said that. He felt them watching him with anxiety that matched his own.

'Maybe when it started to snow heavily she had the common sense to drive to a hotel and check in there for the night?' Phil suggested. 'That's what I'd do.'

'She'd have rung to let me know she was okay!' protested Jenny. 'She would know I'd be worried sick if I didn't hear.'

'If the phones were working, maybe—but some phone lines are down; they said so on the TV news.'

Ross sighed. 'Maybe I should call the police again?'

Jenny nodded. 'The number of our local station is written on that pad beside the phone.'

The desk sergeant Ross talked to was quietly reassuring. 'There is probably a good reason why she hasn't rung. I expect she is safe somewhere, sir, don't think the worst. In weather like this the wisest thing is to get off the road; in fact some roads in the district are quite impassable. We've had to close them to stop drivers getting themselves bogged down in snow. We haven't heard of any accidents involving your wife or her car. I'll certainly alert all our cars to keep an eye open for her, but as you can imagine we're stretched to our limit at the moment. There isn't much else I can do.'

'She could have had an accident somewhere else, *en route*, of course,' Ross thought aloud.

'Yes, that's certainly possible. I'll circulate a description of the car to other areas and see if they have any news. If we hear anything you can be sure we'll ring at once, but take my advice, go to bed and try to sleep. I'm sure you'll have good news in the morning.'

When Ross relayed this to Jenny and her husband Phil

nodded. 'I think he's right. We can't do anything else tonight. We might as well get some sleep. Now, Jen, be sensible—come to bed. Ross, we got the spare room ready for Dylan—you know where it is. I think you should turn in too. You look dead on your feet.'

Shaking his head, Ross said wearily, 'I couldn't rest for a second while I don't know what's happened to her.' Guilt was burning in his stomach. That morning Dylan had begged him not to leave her, pleaded with him to take her with him, and he had refused. He wouldn't even listen to her, he had brushed her worries aside as typical female jitters, not taken her seriously.

He wished to God he could turn the clock back and have a second chance. If anything had happened to her he would never forgive himself.

'I'll be up later,' Jenny told her husband, who gave her a wry look before turning away.

'Don't sit up all night fretting, Jen. It won't do Dylan any good, you know,' he said as he left the room.

Ross was staring at the Christmas tree, watching the fairy lights, gazing at the silver bells and delicate glass birds, red, yellow and blue, which nested in the pine branches.

The scent of the tree reminded him of his own home, of the forest he loved so much, the tall, cathedral-like acres of pines, the dark shadow beneath them, haunting and mysterious. God, he wished he was there now, with Dylan, all this misery and guilt forgotten. If only he hadn't gone off to the conference in York! If only he had taken notice of Dylan's anxiety, stayed home with her as she'd asked!

His tall, lithe body was heavy with exhaustion, his hard-featured face pale, his mouth taut.

'Have you eaten? Can I get you something?' Jenny gently offered.

He shook his head. 'I'm not hungry.'

'Cup of tea or coffee?'

'No, I'm fine, thanks.'

Firmly, Jenny said, 'Well, I'm making some tea—if I don't do something I'll go crazy! I can't bear sitting here doing nothing while she's somewhere out there, maybe dying of hypothermia. Even if she's in her car she'll be getting colder and colder and—' She broke down, sobbing, tears beginning to run down her face. 'Oh, Ross, I'm so scared for her…'

He pulled a paper tissue from a box on the table and dried her face, his arm around her heaving shoulders.

'Don't, Jen. I'm sure she's okay. The police are right; she isn't stupid, she has probably found shelter somewhere—in a hotel, or someone's house. As soon as it's daylight I'll start driving around to look for her myself. Someone is bound to have noticed that crazy car of hers. How could you miss it?' He was trying to talk himself into believing that.

Jenny gave a shaky giggle. 'That's true. Typical of Michael to paint it with all those psychedelic flowers!'

Ross's brows jerked together, his face suddenly harsh. 'Was he into drugs, do you think? I always suspected…'

'Who, Michael? Good heavens, no. He was a fitness freak, obsessed with taking care of his body, watching everything he ate or drank, spending hours working out. He did yoga, not drugs!' Jenny gave Ross a thoughtful look. 'You weren't jealous of him, were you?'

'Jealous?' Ross laughed shortly. 'Of that guy? You're kidding.' His face stiffened. 'You don't think she could have gone to him, do you?'

'She can't have—he's still in America on tour.'

'So he is. I'd forgotten.' Ross gave a brief, unconscious sigh, then looked at her, forcing a pale smile. 'Could we have that tea now, Jenny? And maybe you could rustle me up a sandwich or something? I didn't feel hungry, but I've just realised I haven't eaten all day.'

'Of course I will,' she promised, bustling off.

Dylan was already in bed by then, in Ruth's spare bedroom, floating on a feather mattress which made her feel as if she was sinking into a cloud. Ruth had lit a fire of logs and pine cones in the small, white-painted iron grate to warm the room properly, and for an hour after Dylan went to bed the black reflection of the flames danced on walls and ceiling.

The fire had begun to die down but the faint red glow from the ashes was comforting, as was the soft whisper as from time to time ash drifted down through the iron grating into the pan below. Central heating did not give you the same frisson of pleasure, thought Dylan dreamily, floating off into sleep.

The only thing that would make this experience complete would be to have Ross in bed with her.

If only she wasn't pregnant. If only her body was the way it had been when they first met. She ached to have Ross's hands stroking, caressing her, his mouth brushing her skin, kissing her eyes, her mouth, her neck, travelling down to her naked breasts, his lips parting to let his tongue torment her nipples, before he sucked each into his mouth, his fingers sliding down between her thighs... Sensual images made her toss in the bed, hot with desire and frustration.

What was the point in remembering? At this very moment Ross was probably in bed with Suzy, in York, and she could be sure he wasn't thinking about *her*. She couldn't bear to imagine what he was thinking about, let alone what he and Suzy were doing.

How long had it been going on? Jealousy stabbed inside her. How could Ross do this to her when she was carrying his child? How could he do it to Alan, the man he called his best friend?

Was Suzy behind the change in the way he had been acting these past few months? She had believed he was no longer interested in her because she no longer had the sort of body that had excited him when they were first married.

Sex had been terrific in those early days—was sex all he was interested in? Hadn't he ever really loved her? Loved *her*, in every way, the way she loved him—mind, heart and body, every part of him. Had Ross only ever loved having sex with her?

She turned over again, biting her lower lip in anguish. She had to stop thinking about him, thinking about anything—she was so tired; she had to get some sleep.

She had been to meditation classes years ago, when she was dancing. It had been Michael's idea. He was very into yoga and meditation, he believed a healthy mind meant a healthy body, and she had found the meditation techniques very helpful in preparing her before the curtain went up. You could reach a place of calm where nothing could touch you.

She went through some of those techniques now, emptying her mind, letting her entire body relax, sinking into a state of tranquillity which very gradually became sleep.

Ross made a phone call while Jenny was in the kitchen creating a sandwich for him. 'Suzy? Look, I'm sorry I had to go. Dylan has got herself lost...'

'Lost? What on earth…?' the warm female voice exclaimed at the other end of the line.

'She set off to visit her sister and never arrived, but we haven't heard a word from her. There's probably a perfectly simple explanation, but it's worrying. Sorry to let you down, though.'

'Forget it. No problem, darling—of course you had to go; I understand. I hope you find her soon. Be in touch when you can, Ross.'

Hearing Jenny coming, Ross hurriedly said, 'Yes, I will. Got to go now, Suzy. See you soon.'

Jenny came in, her eyes enquiring, anxious. 'Any news?'

He shook his head. 'Work, I'm afraid. I had to ring a colleague.'

Jenny frowned. 'How can you even think of work at a time like this? Anything could have happened to Dylan…yet you still have work on your mind! Sometimes men make me so angry…'

Placatingly, Ross asked her, 'Is that my sandwich? Looks great—what's in it?'

'Everything,' Jenny said, distracted, as he had hoped. 'Ham, tomato, lettuce, hard-boiled egg, cheese, all bound together with mayonnaise—cheese doesn't keep you awake, does it? Take it out if you're not happy eating it.'

'It never bothers me. In any case I doubt if I'll get much sleep tonight.'

'No,' Jenny said, sighing. 'Oh, where can she be, Ross? I mean, if she did have an accident, why haven't the police heard about it?'

He finally persuaded Jenny to go to bed at midnight, but he sat up in front of the TV until he fell asleep, shallowly, fitfully, in a cramped position, and dreamt of making love to someone: a silky body in his arms, smooth thighs which parted to allow him into a hot, pulsing heaven.

Shuddering and groaning, he woke up to find it was dawn, a strange, white dawn, the reflected light of snow flickering across Ross's eyelids. Morning! He looked at his watch and saw it was seven o'clock. Sitting up, body stiff, mouth dry, he remembered the dream with guilty intensity. His body and his mind seemed to exist on different planets. How could he have dreamt like that when he was feeling so bad about Dylan?

On tiptoe, making as little noise as possible so as not to wake the others in the house, he collected his overnight bag from the hall and went into the downstairs cloakroom to freshen up. Ten minutes later, in a clean shirt, faced shaved and washed, hair combed, feeling a little more human, he went into the kitchen to make himself some black coffee and a slice of toast.

By seven-thirty he was creeping out of the house, leaving a note for Jenny telling her he was going to drive up to the M6 motorway exit Dylan would probably have used to see if he could find any trace of her or her car. He couldn't believe that a vehicle like the flower wagon could vanish without trace. Someone would have seen it.

At first he stayed on main roads, which had been swept by snow ploughs that morning and had a covering of grit; Ross glanced up side roads as he slowly drove by, but reached the motorway exit without any sighting of the flower wagon.

At nine o'clock he stopped to buy a local map in a garage and asked the man behind the desk if he had seen a very pregnant woman driving a car covered in flowers.

He got a very odd look. 'Covered in flowers? A hearse, you mean?'

Ross laughed curtly. 'No, I meant a car painted with a lot of flowers, all the colours of the rainbow.'

'Oh, I get you—no, can't say I have. Think I'd have noticed if a car like that had come in for petrol.'

A postman had come in to hand a packet of mail over. He turned to stare at Ross with curiosity.

'I saw a car like that, half an hour ago—abandoned just outside Stonelee. Stolen, was it? Looked to me as if whoever was driving it had crashed.'

Ross felt his heart stop and then start beating again, so fast he was giddy. 'Crashed?' he repeated hoarsely.

'It had been driven into a wall. Don't worry, the damage isn't really serious, I'd say—scratches and bumps, mainly.'

'Can you tell me where to find it?' Ross opened the map he had just bought and spread it on the counter, his hands shaking. The postman leaned over to point.

'Down that road—it's a tiny lane, and still icy, so be careful. I'm not surprised they crashed your car; I nearly crashed myself. I skated down rather than drove. Lucky my brakes are good.

Ross thanked him and hurried off. He found the flower wagon twenty minutes later and parked behind it. Getting out, he looked around, and immediately noticed the lines of footprints in the snowy field, leading down to the house. He couldn't walk across there in shoes, he would ruin them, and his trousers, too. Opening the back of his four-wheel drive, he fished out the boots he always carried; when you worked in the country you needed to be well prepared for any eventuality.

Locking his vehicle a few minutes later, he set off

down towards the house. As he passed a shed he heard a loud crashing sound, a high-pitched cry, and froze.

That surely wasn't...? Dylan couldn't have spent the night in there?

Hurriedly he opened the door, and reeled back as something rushed out, butting him out of the way. Ross grabbed the door to stop himself falling over, glad he was wearing lined leather gloves.

A goat! he thought, staring after it, then shut the door again before following the previous inhabitant, who by now was down in front of the house, staring through a glass door.

Joining it, Ross stared too, into a pretty kitchen. Was anyone in? he wondered, and tapped loudly on the glass.

There was a blur of blue in the room, someone in a velvet dressing gown walked towards him, and suddenly he couldn't breathe; he felt sick and faint.

She opened the door and stared at him, her eyes wide in surprise.

'Ross!'

He was so relieved he put his arms round her, held her tightly, against his heart, his face buried in her sweet-smelling hair, reminded by the shampoo she had obviously used of the scent of his forest in summer, of pine and fern in sunshine.

She didn't put her arms round him, but her body softened, leaned on his yieldingly, her face against his coat.

But then his mood swung violently. For hours he had been thinking the worst, his head awash with terrifying images of what might have happened to her. He had been rent by guilt and fear. There were so many horrific possibilities—she might have been seriously hurt in a crash, might lose the baby, be maimed, dead, or dying.

And while he was going through hell about her, out

of his mind with panic, she had been safe, here, in this cosy house, all the time.

Angry blood rushed to his head. He reddened, pushed her away and stared down accusingly, shouting at her. 'How could you be so stupid? What on earth possessed you to drive all this way, on one of the worst nights of the winter, in that silly little car of yours? It's a sardine can, even if it is painted with flowers—just a flimsy piece of tin, that damned car! You could have been killed. God knows why you weren't!'

'Don't yell at me!' Dylan threw back, just as furious, just as flushed, and trembling because a moment ago she had been in his arms again, had felt his mouth moving against her hair with a tenderness he had not shown her for a long, long time.

'What do you expect when you behave like a halfwit!' he muttered, staring at her in that soft blue velvet which made her eyes look bluer than ever, the deep warm blue of summer skies.

She was round and swollen as a pumpkin, but she was still very beautiful: her curly hair tied back from her face with a blue velvet scrunchie, her fine features so mobile and expressive that you could read every thought, every emotion unless she deliberately hid them.

He remembered how, when she danced, her body reflected her face, mood and reaction flowing through her throat and breasts, down her arms to her delicate, elegant hands, down through waist, hip and thigh to the long, slim legs. Every inch of her had been eloquent. Then. Until she became pregnant, tethered to the earth, slow-moving, heavy.

He had done that to her. His face darkened with rage and pain and Dylan read his reaction and shivered, looking away. Did he hate her now? Huskily, she asked, 'How did you find me?'

He swallowed, his throat moving visibly. 'Pure coincidence. Jenny rang me in York, because you hadn't arrived at her place, so I drove over here last night. We were up half the night.' His dark grey eyes were glittering points of ice. 'Jenny is out of her mind with worry over you, by the way.'

Her lower lip trembled. 'Oh…poor Jen… I tried to ring but the phone lines are down here.'

He ignored that. 'At first light I started driving around looking for you, and I just happened to meet a postman who had noticed that crazy car of yours!' His tone sharpened to a knife-point. 'Which you had crashed into that wall up there—what were you trying to do, kill yourself and the baby?'

'Don't be so cruel! What a wicked thing to say…even think!' Half in tears, half hating him, she turned on her heel and walked away into the kitchen.

Ross followed, banging the door behind him so that it rattled, but not doing so fast enough. Fred had got in, too, and was making for the heat of the range, standing in front of it, shaking himself.

He lowered his head to enjoy the warmth while showering the entire room with water from the snow that had been drenching his coat as if he had bathed in it. Maybe the stupid animal had rolled in snow, thought Ross, wondering how on earth they would get the goat out of the house.

'Now look what you've done!' Dylan wailed. 'Shoo… Fred…you can't come in. Go out. Shoo.'

Fred ignored her flapping hands and agitated cries, didn't even glance at her.

'He's dripping all over the floor!' she complained.

'And so are you! Take those boots off, for heaven's sake!'

Ross grabbed Fred's leather collar and heaved him towards the door, with Fred wriggling and digging his heels in every inch of the way. Ross was stronger, however; he finally pushed Fred out, slamming the door behind him. Fred glared viciously over his shoulder, his yellowy-blue eyes homicidal, then charged away, up the garden, and butted the shed walls, making them shiver violently.

'You just have to be firm with animals,' Ross said.

Dylan grabbed a mop from a cupboard and dealt with the wet marks of Fred's hooves and Ross's boots. 'If Ruth gets back to see her floor in this mess she'll be furious. Fred isn't allowed indoors; he eats everything, even dishcloths.'

Ross took the mop away from her and finished the work. 'You shouldn't be doing that, not in your condition...and who's Ruth?'

Crossly, Dylan said, 'I've been doing my housework all through my pregnancy—I'm not going to collapse because I mop a wet floor! And will you please take those boots off?'

He rinsed the mop out in the kitchen sink, shook it, then put it away in the cupboard where she had found it, the wet head upwards. Then he pulled off his boots and stood them on the kitchen mat by the door.

Dylan sat down by the table, trembling and feeling sick. 'This is Ruth's house. After I crashed she took me in—she's a very nice woman; she's been very kind to me.' Her blue eyes lifted to his face, dark with reproach, telling him silently that he had not been kind yesterday morning, before he left for York.

Ross felt a familiar stab of guilt, but anger drowned

it out. She had risked her life and that of their baby in
a fit of temper because he had gone away for one night—
if anyone felt guilty it should be Dylan herself. It was
only by pure luck that she had survived that crash. It
could have been fatal.

'Does she live here alone?'

'Yes, she isn't married. She lived here with her widowed mother until the mother died—poor Ruth. I think
she must be very lonely; she doesn't seem to have any
friends. Her phone was out of order all night, or I would
have rung Jenny, to tell her what had happened. It's still
dead this morning, so Ruth is walking to the village to
try to get the garage to come and get my car back on
the road.'

'The roads are like ice rinks,' snapped Ross. 'Let's
hope she makes it safely to the village. I suppose it never
occurred to you that that walk could be dangerous for
her? How old is she, this Ruth?'

Dylan bit her lip, knowing there was some truth in
what he had said. She should never have let Ruth leave.

Defiantly, though, she told him, 'She's not old! In her
forties. And of course I tried to talk her out of going!
You don't think I asked her to go? I told her it would
be better to wait until the phone was working again, but
she had run out of bread and milk and she said she
would have gone to the village even if I hadn't been
here.'

'And you really think she was telling the truth?' he
grated, frowning. 'Anyone with any sense is staying indoors this morning and waiting for a thaw. That's where
I would be if you hadn't forced me to come looking for
you!'

'Don't tell me you give a damn what happens to me!'

she muttered, not looking at him. 'If you had cared you would never have left me alone in that house!'

He ran a hand through his thick dark hair, face tense with guilt and anger at himself which somehow converted into anger with her. 'Dylan, it was an important meeting. I needed to be there. As it was, in the end, I had to leave before it started, to come searching for you! So you won—okay? You won! I hope that makes you happy.'

She looked at him with angry reproach in her eyes. 'It wasn't a win-lose situation, Ross! I was scared; I needed you.'

He groaned. 'I'm sorry, Dylan. I believed the forecasts. I didn't think the weather would deteriorate so fast. I wish I'd listened to you.'

'You only had to look at the sky, those clouds, feel the way the temperature was dropping!'

'I know. I admit it. You were right; I was wrong. Your instincts were better than mine, as far as the weather was concerned.' He was trying to soften her mood, but his anxiety and fury with her surfaced again a second later. 'A pity you were so stupid about not staying put in the house!' he burst out. 'You were much safer there—what on earth put it into your head to drive off to visit your sister without even letting me know you were going?'

She looked bitterly at him, eyes dark as night skies. 'Does Suzy mean anything to you?'

'Suzy?' he repeated, face changing, no doubt with consternation. He didn't say anything else—he was giving himself time to think, not sure how much she knew.

'Oh, don't bother to lie! She rang you on your mobile just before lunch yesterday. Of course I answered it, and before I got a word out she was talking. Purring, actually, like some cat on heat.' she bitterly imitated the other woman, her face flickering with pretended sweetness. '"Ross, darling, Alan hasn't left yet so I can't get away to meet you!"'

It hadn't occurred to him that Suzy might have rung him earlier, especially on his mobile—she hadn't mentioned having done so when they'd talked later on the hotel phone.

Eyes hard, grim, he bit out, 'So you jumped to the worst possible conclusions, decided I was having an affair? But you didn't ring me at the hotel in York—you didn't wait to ask me what was going on? You just walked out on our marriage. Is that what you're saying?'

'What marriage?' she fiercely counter-attacked, leaning forward over the kitchen table, trying to disguise the shaking of her body.

She wouldn't give him the satisfaction of seeing how hurt and jealous she was, for one thing, and for another her back was aching badly, a deep, persistent, nagging pain which was getting worse by the minute and making it hard to think. Backache had been a frequent part of being pregnant this last few months, but it had never been as bad as this before.

Bitterly, she asked Ross, 'When was the last time you kissed me? Made love to me? Even held me? Is that what you call marriage?'

He exploded. 'For God's sake! You're heavily pregnant, Dylan! I was trying to be thoughtful...'

'Thoughtful?' she threw back at him, laughing hoarsely. 'You're kidding! Is that what you call it? You think it's thoughtful to treat me like a leper just because I'm pregnant?'

He was as angry now as she was, his voice harsh. 'Ella warned me not to try to make love to you in the last few months. She said you wouldn't feel like it and it might harm the baby!'

Dylan sat very still, staring at him, mouth open incredulously. 'Ella said what?'

At that second they both heard footsteps outside, boots crunching on the crystal surface of the snow. Looking round, they saw Ruth staring at them through the glass door, great white flakes of snow blowing behind her.

Dumbly Dylan thought, 'It's snowing again. That's all I need.

Opening the door, Ruth asked sharply, 'Who's this, Dylan? What's he doing here?'

Realising Ruth suspected Ross of being an intruder, Dylan stammered, 'This is my—my husband, Ross. Ross, this is Ruth Nicholls.'

Ross offered Ruth his hand. 'Hello, Ruth. Thank you for taking such good care of my wife—we're very grateful for everything you've done for her.'

Ruth inspected him curiously, eyes still cool and speculative. 'Hello. How did you find out she was here? Is the phone working again, Dylan?'

'I don't think so.' Dylan found it hard to concentrate on anything. Her back hurt too much. And she kept thinking about what Ross had told her just before Ruth arrived. His sister had told him not to make love to her? Ella had had no business saying any such thing.

'I started looking for her at first light,' Ross said. 'And after a few hours I met a postman who, amazingly, had noticed her car up there on the lane. It was an astonishing stroke of luck.'

Ruth laughed. 'Country districts are like that—everyone notices everything. I'm afraid I couldn't get the garage to come and look at her car. They're run off their feet today. Dylan wasn't the only one to have a crash, and the garage are dealing with their own customers first, but they promised to try to come tomorrow, if the roads are clear around here. At the moment, the back roads like this one are all no-go areas, I'm afraid.'

'And I see it is snowing again. Is it heavy?'

'I'm afraid so. It looks to me as if it is going to go on all day.'

'Well, I think we should go at once, then,' Ross said flatly. 'Dylan's sister lives about eight miles from here. Not far in normal weather, but in heavy snow it could take an hour or so.'

Dylan stood up shakily. 'I'd better go and dress, then.' Ruth had brought her case in from the flower wagon just after breakfast, so she now had fresh clothes to put on.

'I'll come with you to talk,' Ross said ominously, and she shook her head hurriedly. She needed time to think before she was alone with him.

'No, stay and talk to Ruth. I'm going to take a shower.'

She caught Ruth's startled glance but didn't let their eyes meet. Ruth knew she had already had a bath that morning.

Ross didn't try to insist, to her relief. Shrugging, he said, 'Okay, don't be long. I want to get away before this snow makes the roads treacherous.'

As she began making her way upstairs she heard him say to Ruth, 'I've got a four-wheel drive, it can cope with any weather or terrain, and her sister is waiting anxiously to see her. Thank you again for…'

Dylan slipped into the spare bedroom and closed the door with a sigh of mingled relief, pain and confusion.

Was Ross telling the truth? Had his sister really told him not to sleep with her? It explained so much that had been hurting her, puzzling her, all these weeks past. Why on earth hadn't Ross told her what Ella had said, though? If she had known, everything would have been so different.

She took a step towards the wardrobe where she had hung her clothes and doubled up with a grunt of agony as the pain in her back moved round to the front with a stabbing intensity unlike any pain she had ever felt in her life.

Groaning, she sank down on the bed, head down, trying to breathe the way she had been taught, fighting to regain control of her body in a struggle with the pain attempting to dominate it.

It subsided and she slackened in relief. Oooh, that was better. At least she could think again now.

How long had she had this back pain? Hours. Why on earth hadn't she recognised it? She had read all about giving birth, she had been to antenatal clinic every month, she had talked to her midwife and doctor about what to expect...but she had totally missed one of the classic symptoms!

She had been so preoccupied with Ross, with her jealousy, her uncertainty, her hurt feelings, that she had not realised she was in labour.

She must have been in labour for a long time; the question was how much longer would it take? She was booked into a maternity hospital in the borders—much too far away. She would never get there in time, especially on roads blocked with snow, even if Ross tried to get her there.

The pain jabbed again, deep inside her, so painful that she could not sit still. She got up to walk about, trying to distract herself from it, breathing while she stared at her watch. How long since the last contraction? She had no idea—she hadn't noticed the time.

She would have to wait until the next pain started and time from that; that would give her some idea how advanced she was in labour.

The door opened and Ross came in, stopped dead, staring at her. 'What the hell are you doing, walking about like that?'

She told him and saw his face go white.

'You can't be having it now! There's another month to go!'

'You tell the baby that,' Dylan said, sitting down again as the pain quietened and letting out a long, weary sigh of relief. 'Could you drive over to Ruth's friend Henry and ask him to come?'

'What? Who?' echoed Ross, looking at her as if she was nuts.

She laughed, feeling light-headed. 'He's a doctor.'

'Right, okay,' Ross said, turning and disappearing at speed. She heard him crashing down the stairs, his voice urgently talking to Ruth below in the kitchen.

She was surprised when he came back almost at once. 'The phones are working again—Ruth has rung Henry but he is out on another call. His nurse said she would give him the message, but I think I should drive you to the nearest hospital.'

The pain had her in its vicious grip again by then; she closed her eyes, breathing rhythmically.

When she could speak again she whispered, dark-eyed with pain, 'No. No, I can't. It hurts so much, Ross, and the pains are coming faster and closer together. I don't think there is time to drive to hospital.'

CHAPTER EIGHT

'BUT you can't have the baby here!' Ross's voice was harsh, his face tense. 'It wouldn't be safe. You'll need help, a midwife, a doctor…someone who knows what they're doing. A first-time mother has to have her baby in hospital.'

Dylan rubbed her back, face defiant. 'No, I'm not risking a long drive. The pains come too close together; I'd be scared of having the baby arrive before I got to hospital.' She groaned, sweat breaking out on her forehead. 'If only the doctor would get here!'

Ross sat down next to her and turned sideways on so that he could massage her back. Dylan felt his strong, warm, muscular hands stroking firmly, rhythmically, pressing into her tense muscles, and sighed, relaxing, closing her eyes.

'That's wonderful.'

He went on kneading her, murmuring close to her ear, his voice persuasive, 'Dylan, listen, you have to be sensible. I'll drive you very slowly and carefully, I promise. Let me take you to the nearest hospital. You'll be risking the baby's life if you don't, not to mention your own. I couldn't bear it if anything went wrong.'

'Why should you care? The way you've been treating me the last few months!' she muttered, but knew he might be right. Maybe it would be wiser to go to the hospital? If only she had a clearer idea what to expect!

But she stopped thinking as the pain came surging back. She had to relax, so that she could do her breathing exercises, but she had been taken off guard and her body was too tense, fighting the pain instead of going with it.

'Lean on me,' said Ross, putting an arm round her and gently stroking her taut abdomen the way he had her back.

She let herself slump against him, surrendering to his hands, and her breathing slowed, deepened. The pleasure of having Ross touching her with such tenderness helped. When the pain went she stayed very still, not wanting him to stop. It had been so long since they had had such intimate contact.

There was a tap on the door at that moment, and Ruth asked, 'May I come in?'

'Of course, please do. We could use your advice,' Ross said, relief in his voice. 'She seems to be in a lot of pain.'

Ruth came in, looking sharply at Dylan, eyes skimming her from head to toe. 'Is it really bad, Dylan?'

She nodded, saving her breath.

Ruth said, 'I just tried to ring for an ambulance but there's no bed available in the local hospital—they said there was no point in bringing you in as they had no-where to put you. They suggested trying other hospitals in the area but they said your doctor should do that, so until Henry gets here there's nothing else to be done, I'm afraid.'

'The pains are coming every few minutes; she must be well into labour,' Ross said flatly. 'Unless this doctor friend of yours arrives soon we may find ourselves de-livering the baby.'

Looking aghast, Ruth said, 'How soon do you think the baby will arrive, Dylan?'

'I don't know! I never had a baby before!' Dylan

heard the ring of panic in her own voice and tried to sound calmer. 'There must be a local midwife, surely!'

'Of course, and I already tried her number, but she was out on another call, too. I left a message on her answer-machine.'

'We must do something!' Ross broke out fiercely.

Dylan stopped listening to them. The process gripping her body made everyone else around her unimportant for a minute or two.

By noon the white snow blew in swirls and drifts which blotted out the leaden sky. An arctic wind rattled the bare branches in the garden; it seemed colder today than it had been yesterday. Even Fred was happy to stay locked in the shed with a net of hay to eat, and Cleo slept, curled nose to tail, in front of the glowing range in between visits upstairs to investigate the comings and goings of her owner and the two visitors.

'Stay out of here,' Ruth told her the third time, firmly shooing her out.

Green eyes slitted, black tail lashing, Cleo peered past into the bedroom at the woman making yowling noises on the bed.

'She knows what's going on,' Ruth said drily. 'She's kittened twice.'

'A pity she can't talk, then. We could ask her advice!' Ross groaned.

Dylan laughed, perspiration-dampened hair clinging to her hot forehead. 'She probably thinks I'm making a big fuss over nothing.'

Ruth laughed. 'I don't know about that. Cats hate being undignified, and giving birth is not a dignified process! She probably feels sorry for you.'

Ross wiped Dylan's face with a cool, damp flannel.

'Where the hell is that doctor? Could you try him again, Ruth?'

'I just did but the phone lines are down again—not surprising with this wind howling. Maybe one day this country will bury all the phone lines underground and put an end to these winter problems. It's the same every winter.'

'You would choose to give birth just when we're having the worst weather of the year,' Ross said to Dylan, softly brushing her damp hair back from her face in rhythmic movements which were very soothing.

For such a big, powerful man he could be amazingly gentle. Dylan loved having him there, looking after her; he made it much easier to bear what was happening.

At that moment a male voice downstairs called out. 'Ruth? Are you up there?'

'Oh...the doctor...' sighed Dylan, and Ross's face lit up with weary relief.

'Thank God for that! I was beginning to think he'd never get here.'

Ruth hurried out of the room. They heard her call down the stairs, 'Yes, come up, Henry. Thank heavens you got here!'

She and Henry murmured together on the landing, their voices not quite audible, and then Henry came into the bedroom, his shrewd eyes assessing Dylan's condition briefly before moving on to examine Ross.

'Hello, there! You're the husband, right? Glad you're here with your wife. It always helps to have a father on call for support and comfort. But just for the moment I need to see your wife alone—why don't you go downstairs for a few minutes while I examine her? I need to see just how far advanced she is before I decide what to do. You look as if you could do with a break, too. A trying business, childbirth. It can take a lot out of a fellow. Why don't you make us all a cup of tea? I could do with one, myself.'

Ross glared back at him, saying fiercely, 'I want you to find her a hospital bed. She can't have the baby here; it isn't safe. If anything goes wrong there won't be anything we can do about it.'

Henry soothed him, using his best bedside manner. 'Normally, of course, you're a hundred per cent right. A first-time mother should be in a maternity ward, being looked after by a midwife, with lots of nursing back-up and all the most up-to-date equipment on hand for emergencies.'

'Then get on the phone and find her a bed somewhere!'

'I've already tried to find a bed—the nearest available one is thirty miles off...'

'Thirty miles!' interrupted Dylan, face agitated. 'No, I won't go all that way, jolting about in an ambulance on dangerous roads.'

Henry gave her a rueful look. 'My dear girl, there is no chance whatever of an ambulance driving here. They have too many medical emergencies to cope with. It's a battlefield out there. The roads are littered with abandoned cars. Every operating theatre is working flat out. A woman having a baby is not a priority case, I'm afraid, unless her life, or the baby's, is in real danger.'

Ross broke out, 'I'll drive her there. My car is a four-wheel drive; it can cope with these conditions.'

'No!' Dylan shook her head in terror. 'It's too dangerous.'

Henry made a face. 'She's right. It just took me over half an hour to get here. The roads are murder; I had to drive at a snail's pace and my tyres wouldn't grip on the mixture of ice and new snow. I kept skidding and slid-ing—it was like trying to drive on a skating rink.'

Impatiently, Ross insisted, his voice rising harshly, 'I'll get her there, somehow!'

'No,' Dylan groaned. 'Please, Ross! Stop shouting. Haven't I got enough problems without you being so belligerent and throwing your weight around?'

He looked at her uncertainly, his hands screwed up at his sides.

Henry studied her, face expressionless. 'Your wife is right. She has enough to cope with, just giving birth, and she's frightened. I understand how worried you are, but you'll just have to face the fact that we can't get her to a hospital yet. But we'll manage somehow. Off you go and make that tea while I examine her, then I can give you a better idea of the situation we're facing.'

'I want the truth!' Ross grated, scowling.

'You'll get it,' Henry promised.

Ross looked at Dylan, trailed his fingers across her limp brown curls without a word, then went out.

She sighed. 'I'm sorry he was so aggressive.'

'Oh, I'm quite used to bad-tempered fathers-in-waiting,' Henry said jovially. 'The old tradition was for them to go to the pub and drink while their wives got on with it, which was quite useful because they were rarely much use and only got in the way.'

'Well, I'd rather have him here than down at the pub!'

'Of course you would. You need him, I know,' soothed Henry. 'In the old days it was much easier if you had a granny or an older sister helping out; they knew what to do and were often as good as a trained nurse. Today, the father is expected to share every stage of the birth, and some of them find the whole process terrifying. I've had them pass out! One young lad fainted on top of his unfortunate wife just as I was actually delivering their baby. I didn't know which one to catch first.'

Dylan laughed. 'Oh, I'm sure Ross won't do that! He's been wonderful, hasn't he, Ruth? He's coping better than I am! I'm afraid I'm not very brave.'

'With first mothers fear is the worst enemy. They don't know what to expect so they panic a bit. Easy to understand. You're always afraid of what you don't know,' said Henry. 'Well, let's see how your baby is doing.' He smiled at Ruth. 'Is that a hot water bottle in bed with her?'

'It helped her backache, and I thought it might help the pain—wasn't it the right thing to do?'

'Of course it was. Don't often see them in modern houses, with all this central heating, but they are a real boon. I can warm my stethoscope before I put it on her tummy. It can be quite a shock to the system, a chilly stethoscope, especially in this sort of weather.'

By the time Ross brought up a tray of tea Henry had finished his examination and was talking quietly to Ruth while Dylan lay back with closed eyes, resting after her latest contraction.

Ross's hard grey eyes flashed to her, then moved on to Henry, his brows lifting anxiously.

'Is she okay?'

'She's fine—she's doing very well.'

Ross's tension relaxed a little. 'And the baby?'

'Baby's fine, too—positioned perfectly for a straightforward birth. Don't worry. Dylan is a strong, fit girl, with excellent muscle tone. I gather she is a trained dancer, so she could cope very well with giving birth,' Henry told him in a reassuring voice. 'It won't be long now—another hour or so, I'd say—and I don't anticipate any serious problems at all.'

Ross gave a long, audible sigh of relief. Ruth poured the tea and handed Henry his cup.

'Have you had lunch?' she asked him, observing the tired lines around his pale eyes, the weary droop of his lips.

He shook his head. 'Not yet, and I'm starving. I've been working flat out for most of the last couple of days; I've had very little sleep and not much to eat, either.'

'I could heat up some soup and grill a steak for you.'

His face brightened. 'Would you, Ruth? That sounds wonderful; I would love a steak. I don't suppose you've got mushrooms and tomatoes to go with it?'

Her eyes amused and affectionate, she nodded. 'Of course—and some chips?'

'Marvellous. Yes, please!' he said with enthusiasm.

Ruth raised her brows at Ross. 'Does that suit you too? I have plenty of steak in the deep freeze and I've been thawing some of it, which should be ready to cook by now.'

'Thanks, that would be terrific.'

Henry cheerfully told Dylan, 'Afraid you can't join us—eating interferes with the birth process. Can't have food being digested while baby is trying to be born.'

'I couldn't eat anyway. I'm not hungry.' Dylan looked across the bedroom at the window, where snow eddied in great white flakes against a sky which had suddenly turned bright blue. 'Look, the sun has come out!' she murmured, her mood lifting a little. Odd how much better you felt when the sun was shining. Why was that?

After Ross had finished his meal he went back upstairs to sit with Dylan while Henry and Ruth sat in the kitchen drinking coffee.

'You're looking a little better now. You obviously

needed blood sugar,' Ruth said, watching the ruthless sunlight picking out deep-bitten lines in his face.

'I'm old,' he said without regret.

'Nonsense! You're nothing of the kind! Middle-aged, that's all.'

He grinned at her. 'What a nice woman you are! Why didn't you ever marry when you were young, Ruth?'

She looked out of the window, a little sadness in her eyes. 'Oh, there was this boy, when I was eighteen... He was called Joe; I'd known him most of my life. He lived at Oak Farm, we saw a lot of each other one summer, fell in love. We got engaged and planned to get married the following spring. His parents were pleased; they offered us one of the farm cottages. My mother started planning the wedding. We had a little holiday together, just a weekend, staying with his older sister at Scarborough. One morning he got up very early and went for a swim. The water was very cold. He drowned.'

'How terrible,' Henry said heavily. 'What a waste of a life.'

Ruth sighed. 'Yes, it was a waste, and so stupid. It need never have happened. He was never a strong swimmer. I don't know what made him go to the beach on his own at that hour. It seems he got cramp—a local fisherman saw he was in trouble, and tried to save him, but Joe went under before the man got to him.'

Henry watched her, face thoughtful. 'Have you been mourning him all this time?'

She started, looked at him with a wry little smile. 'Oh, no. I was very unhappy for a few years, but time heals everything, doesn't it? No, I haven't thought of Joe for a long time. But somehow I never met anyone else I really cared about. I had the occasional boyfriend, but it never lasted. You see, I'd been so much in love with Joe that I wasn't prepared to settle for anything less. Every time I met someone I suppose I unconsciously measured the way I felt for him against the way I had felt about Joe, and the new man always lost out. Then I was into my thirties, and too busy with my career to think about getting married. It was ironic, really—I had to give up my career anyway, to come back here and look after my mother.'

'You're a wonderful woman, Ruth,' Henry said, and she flushed.

'Oh, nonsense! I couldn't just stick her into a home and let strangers take care of her. I don't regret giving up my life in London and my job for her—although I have to admit I sometimes yearn for city life again. But I expect that at my age I'd hate it now. I shall stay here all my life, I suppose.'

Two hours later, Dylan's baby came into the world. A little girl with a mop of fine, dark hair and a very loud voice. Dylan watched Ruth weigh her, naked and squirming, on kitchen scales covered in kitchen paper.

'Five pounds two ounces!'

'Surprisingly good weight.' Henry had examined the child a few moments ago. 'And she's perfect; she has all her bits and pieces so you don't need to worry about her. She has very good lungs, too—listen to her!'

Dylan laughed. 'I am! Noisy, isn't she?'

'She's gorgeous,' Ruth said, shawling the infant in a clean towel before putting her into her old wicker sewing basket, which was the closest they could come to a cot. Lined with a folded sheet, it was just big enough for the small, swaddled form, and the baby's angry crying stopped as she fell asleep.

Ross had gone downstairs a few minutes earlier to

make a pot of tea while Ruth and Henry dealt with the final stages of the birth.

Watching Ruth's face as she stared down at the baby, Henry asked her, 'Do you ever wish you'd had a child?'

She sighed, giving him a little nod. 'But it never happened, so there's no point in wishing, is there? What about you?'

He smiled at her. 'Yes, I'd have loved it. But Gwen couldn't have one, poor woman. If she'd had one she might have been happier.'

'I don't think Gwen was the contented wife and mother type,' Ruth said drily, then flushed, meeting his eyes. 'Sorry, that sounded catty, didn't it?'

'You never liked her, did you?'

'No,' she said, chin up in defiance. 'And she never liked me.'

Henry laughed. 'Well, she was jealous of you, wasn't she?'

Ruth blinked, eyes opening wide. 'Jealous? Of me? Of course she wasn't—why should she be?'

'I made the mistake of telling her once what a marvellous person I thought you were.' Henry shrugged. 'From then on Gwen loathed you.'

Ross came back at that moment and came over to gaze adoringly at the tiny, red, wrinkled, old man's face which was all he could see by then of his daughter.

'I can't believe how beautiful she is!'

'Isn't she? Just look at all that black hair. I think she's going to take after you, Ross,' said Ruth, then looked from him to his wife. 'What are you going to call her?'

'Ruth,' Dylan said, by now half asleep after all her exertions. She was feeling as light as air, very contented. Her bedclothes had been changed—the new sheets had a clinging, fresh-air smell of lavender—she had been washed, her hair brushed, and was wearing a clean white cotton nightdress.

Flushing, Ruth protested, 'Oh, no! That's very nice of you, but really, there's no need to…'

'I always liked the name Ruth,' said Henry thoughtfully.

Through half-closed eyes, Dylan watched them both. Ruth had flushed, her face suddenly years younger. She likes him a lot, thought Dylan. But does he feel the same about her?

'Ruth "amid the alien corn",' Henry went on. 'That was one of my favourite stories from the Bible at school. She was such a strong woman. After her husband died she didn't abandon her old mother-in-law; she worked hard to keep them both. Faithful and loyal—old-fashioned virtues these days, when too many people put themselves first; we could do with a lot more people like her.'

'This is the "me" generation.' Ross shrugged cynically. 'People have been brought up to believe they should always do what's best for them, never mind what happens to anyone else.'

'This is a sad, bad world,' Henry muttered. 'Thank God there are still a few people like Ruth in it.'

'Ruth is such a lovely name,' Dylan said with a yawn. 'We love it, and we would like you to be her godmother, wouldn't we, Ross?'

They had talked about it while Ruth was cooking lunch; she had done so much for them and they both liked her.

Pink and very touched, Ruth said shyly, 'I'd love that. But what about your own families? Won't they mind?'

'I'm quite sure they won't,' Ross said.

For Dylan the last two days had been hectic, a helter-

skelter ride which took the breath away. She was glad
the birth was over and she had a healthy baby, but she
knew there were still a lot of problems in her life. She
had a lot to talk to Ross about, a lot of questions to ask.
There was still a shadow over their future.

But at that moment her eyelids were as heavy as lead;
she let them close and a moment later was fast asleep.

When she woke up the room was shadowy, only a faint
pink light shining from a fringed lamp on a table by the
window. The curtains were drawn but she realised night
had fallen. Ross sat in an armchair beside the table, a
book open on his lap. He was asleep, face flushed, his
head lolling against the wing of the chair, mouth slightly
open, his breathing slow and regular.

Dylan watched him passionately, her heartbeat quick-
ening, her nipples hard and hot under her thin cotton
nightie. She was taken aback to feel a dampness there
too, and put a hand to her chest, eyes widening.

What on earth was that? For a second or two she was
confused, then it dawned on her—the ache and swell of
her breasts, the slight leakage. Wasn't nature miracu-
lous? As soon as she had had her baby other changes
had begun in her body, so that she could feed the child.

Where was her baby? She sat up, drawing a sharp
breath as she realised how stiff her muscles were; having
a baby was even harder work than dancing a full performance of a ballet. She felt as if she had been working
out for days. Massaging her stomach, she was gratified
to find it flatter again—although it must be flabby now.
As soon as she was up on her feet she must start exercising, strengthen those muscles, make sure her body
returned to its old athletic shape.

Ross stirred, eyes opening slowly, then he sat up, raking back the tousled dark hair which had flopped over his temples, and looked across the room hurriedly.

'You're awake!' He got up, letting the book on his lap fall to the carpet. He bent to pick it up and put it on the arm of the chair before coming over to the bed. 'How do you feel?'

'As if I'd run a hundred miles,' she grimaced, then asked anxiously, 'Where's my baby? Is she okay?'

'She's not just okay, she's a miracle,' Ross said, smiling, and her heart quickened at the sight of that smile. Love hurt inside her, an intolerable, wrenching pain worse than any she had suffered while she gave birth. How could she bear to lose him?

She pushed the agony away, concentrating on what he was saying. 'She's downstairs. We didn't want her crying and waking you up. You needed to sleep.'

Somehow she managed to speak, amazed to hear her voice sound so normal. 'I want to see her, Ross. Please get her for me. I hardly had a chance to see her before I went to sleep.'

Soothingly he said, 'In a minute. First Henry said you must have something to eat and drink, then you can feed little Ruth. He told me to call out when you woke up.'

She looked away from him, trembling. 'What time is it?'

'Ten o'clock. You've been asleep for about six hours. So has the baby. Don't worry. We haven't heard a peep out of her.'

Immediately Dylan stiffened, alarm in her eyes. 'There could be something wrong!'

'Don't get so agitated! I told you, she's fine—Ruth and Henry take a look at her every so often to make sure she's okay. Now, just lie still while I call Henry.'

'He stayed here all day?'

'No, he had to go out on calls, but he got back half an hour ago and came up to check on you while Ruth cooked his supper. I don't know how he keeps going. He only just managed to get here this time—the roads are atrocious now, apparently. His partner is going to do the night shift and Ruth has persuaded him to stay overnight.'

'What about you? You must need some sleep, too.'

He looked at her through his lashes, his mouth mocking. 'I can share your bed, can't I?'

Her flush grew hectic, blue eyes darkening as the pupils dilated. 'That isn't funny!'

'It wasn't meant to be! We may not be able to make love for a while but there's no reason why I shouldn't sleep in the same bed, is there?'

'No!' she said fiercely, voice shaking. 'You aren't sharing my bed; you can't have both me and your mistress!'

His face turned grim and he came towards the bed with a loping tread like a jungle cat, a jaguar, big and dark and menacing, making her heart leap into her mouth.

'I haven't got a mistress!' he said through clenched teeth.

She lifted her chin defiantly, out-staring him, jealousy and pain in her face and voice. 'Did you think I'd forgotten about her? Having the baby hasn't softened my brain or made me lose my memory, Ross. You said you hadn't been making love to me because your sister told you not to! But I know the truth, don't I? You haven't been interested in me because you've been having an affair with Suzy!'

In the same clipped, harsh voice, he snapped, 'You

can't seriously believe I'd do something like that to my best friend!'

Staring with shock and contempt at Ross, she accused, 'I know what I heard! Suzy thought it was you answering your mobile. She called you darling, whispered in a furtive sort of way, saying she couldn't leave yet because Alan was still around but she was looking forward to that night…it was obvious what was going on! And it will kill Alan when he finds out she's been having an affair with you!'

'She hasn't!' he angrily shot back, face darkly flushed and brows heavy over his hard grey eyes. 'There is no affair—it's all in your imagination!'

'Don't lie to me, Ross! Why else would she say she couldn't leave because she didn't want Alan to suspect anything? What else could that mean?'

'She didn't want him to guess what we were planning!'

Dylan laughed scornfully. 'I bet she didn't!'

Curtly, Ross said, 'Will you listen? It was Alan's birthday yesterday and we were organising a big birthday party for him at the hotel in York!'

Shaken, Dylan stared up at him, eyes hunting over his clenched face before she slowly asked, 'If that's true, why didn't you ever mention this party to me?'

'Because I couldn't take you and I didn't want to upset you by talking about a party you couldn't go to!'

Tears burnt behind her lids. 'You couldn't take me because if I saw you with her I might guess what was going on!'

'For God's sake! Nothing has been going on between me and Suzy! She loves Alan…'

'Is that why she picks on him all the time, criticises him in public, makes fun of him?'

Ross sighed. 'Yes. I wish she wouldn't treat him like that, but she does love him, Dylan. It's just her nature, all that sniping. Alan takes it all in good humour.'

'He ought to give her as good as he gets some time! I wouldn't stand for being spoken to the way she talks to him.'

'I know, I agree—but Alan's a slow, quiet chap. He isn't the aggressive type. He adores her.' Ross looked at Dylan soberly. 'Dylan, I wouldn't hurt Alan for the world, and I have never been interested in Suzy. She's fun, she's very attractive—but she isn't my type.'

She wanted so badly to believe him, but she wasn't going to let him make a fool of her. She wanted the truth, the whole truth and nothing but the truth.

'I saw you with her once, sitting in your car, talking, in the forest car park.'

His face was blank. 'When was that?'

'I don't know—back in the autumn. The two of you looked very cosy, as if you were sharing secrets.'

'Are you sure Alan wasn't there? Some time in the autumn he did spend the day in my region; we were marking trees for felling… I remember he brought Suzy with him and we ate our sandwiches together in my car.'

'I didn't see Alan!'

Ross gave her an impatient look. 'When we get back home you can ask Alan himself! If Suzy was there, so was he! I have never met her anywhere alone. Dylan, I'm not having an affair with her!'

'Then why couldn't you take me to the party? If you aren't having an affair, why couldn't I come? I haven't been to a party for months, and you know I love parties.'

He sighed. 'I know you do, darling, but I was afraid the drive to York would be too much for you. This hasn't been an easy pregnancy, has it? I've been very worried about you, especially during the last few weeks, and the doctor warned me that you ought to rest as much as possible over the final month or two. You're so small and delicate.'

'She told me I was as fit as a fiddle. She said I wouldn't have any problems!'

'She lied to you. She didn't want to worry you, and neither did I, but although you were very fit and healthy you were tiny; she thought you might have problems giving birth because your hips are so narrow.'

There was a tap on the door at that second. Startled, they stopped talking and looked across the room as Ruth came in, smiling.

'Oh, good, you are awake! I thought I heard voices.'

What exactly had Ruth heard? They had been shouting at each other, forgetting that there were others in the house. Embarrassed, Dylan flushed, looking away, and couldn't force herself to reply.

'I brought you a cup of tea,' Ruth went on cheerfully, putting the cup down on the bedside table.

'Oh, thank you. I was dying for some tea!'

'Are you hungry, too? You haven't had anything to eat since breakfast—I made a chicken casserole for Henry, with lots of vegetables and some herb dumplings; there's plenty left—could you manage some of it?'

Dylan managed a wavering smile. 'I'd love some, thank you—but first I'd like to go to the bathroom. Am I allowed out of bed?'

'No!' snapped Ross, bristling. 'Don't be ridiculous— you only had the baby eight hours ago. You can't get up yet.'

Gently, Ruth said, 'Well, actually, I did ask Henry when you will be allowed out of bed, and he says he leaves it to the patient. If she feels she wants to get up he lets her. Years ago patients were kept in bed for a week or more, but not any more; the new approach is to get the patient moving again as soon as they feel up to it. So, if you want to try a walk to the bathroom, Dylan, it's okay.'

Dylan slid her legs out from under the covers and stood up a little uncertainly.

Ross jumped to put an arm round her. 'See? You're shaking like a jelly! Get back into bed.'

She shook her head obstinately. 'I'll be fine. It's only a few steps!' She began to walk, feeling as if her legs were made of lead; lifting each foot seemed a tremendous effort, and Ross held on to her, taking some of her weight as she moved. At the bathroom door she pushed him away. 'I can manage alone now, thanks.'

'Well, don't lock the door!' he said tersely as she shut him out.

With the door closed she let herself slacken, leaning on the wall, aware of wobbly legs. She wasn't going to faint, was she? That would convince Ross he was right to treat her as if she was too feeble to move an inch.

Could she believe everything he had just said? Had she put two and two together after Suzy's phone call but got the wrong answer? Had the 'affair' been the product of an over-feverish imagination? Had he and Suzy simply been planning Alan's birthday party?

Going over what Suzy had said again, Dylan realised she could have misunderstood—Ross's explanation might be true.

The trouble was, she wanted so badly to believe him. A tremor of pleasure, of eagerness, ran through her— did he still love her, then? But if he did how could he have been so cool to her these last months? Had her pregnancy turned him off, or was he telling the truth about the advice his sister had given him?

Dylan looked at herself in the mirror assessingly—now that she had had the baby would his desire for her reawaken? How strange her reflection looked without the large bump in the middle of her body she had grown so used to seeing! She flattened her nightie with one hand, and felt a faint flabbiness under her palm. She must start exercising again, get back her muscle tone, get back the figure she had had when she met Ross.

Everything had happened so fast. They had married too quickly, perhaps; she should have realised how big an adaptation she would have to make, but she had been too much in love at the beginning. She hadn't allowed herself to think of anything but a driving need to be with Ross.

Refusing to think too deeply, she had given up her career, her friends, her family, her home. Her entire life had changed overnight, and then her body had begun to change as the child inside her grew.

Now that it was over she could admit to herself how hard it had been to adapt to all those abrupt changes. She should have given herself time to get used to a new way of life before she started the baby—but then she had never planned to get pregnant; it had been an accident.

The pregnancy had been the real problem all along, she recognised. A dancer needed to be light, free, supple—and suddenly she had been none of those things, and she had hated that. Ross was right. Her slight build had made her pregnancy difficult. She had suffered appalling morning sickness for weeks and when that had passed off she had been miserable about her changing shape, had resented getting fat and heavy.

She had blamed Ross for it, hadn't she? Oh, not consciously, but somewhere in her mind he had taken the blame, especially when he'd stopped making love to her and seemed to be avoiding her.

If she had talked to Ross frankly they might have understood each other better, but they hadn't even known each other a year, and Ross had always been so busy. He had been out in the forest during daylight hours, and sometimes during the night. When they were together they hadn't done much talking in the first months of their marriage. Their desire for each other had been too hot, too intense; the fire had flared up the instant they were alone together.

When she'd woken up just now and seen him asleep in that chair she had instantly felt her body burn with passion, with need, with desire. Her own feelings hadn't changed—but had his?

They had to start talking, understand each other at last—there must be no more misunderstandings.

Five minutes later she went back into the bedroom to find Ross alone, standing by the fireplace, putting another log on the fire burning in the grate. The dry wood crackled and a greenish flame shot up the chimney. Hearing her, Ross turned his head without straightening, his thick black hair tumbling over his face.

'Are you okay?'

'I'm fine.'

She had splashed her face with lukewarm water, combed her hair and tied it back from her face. Staring with an awareness that made her pulses beat twice as fast, Ross said huskily, 'You look the way you did when we first met! It suits you, that hairstyle—shows off your beautiful cheekbones and those great big blue eyes.'

She couldn't remember the last time he had paid her

a compliment, or looked at her the way he was looking now! Flushed and breathless, she climbed back into the bed, which either Ross or Ruth had remade while she was in the bathroom. She was relieved to lie down again; the effort of that visit to the bathroom had been more tiring than she had expected.

'Ruth won't be a moment,' he said, still staring, making her very self-conscious. Coming over to the bed, he sat down and picked up her hand, stroking her slender fingers. 'Dylan...you do believe me, now, don't you? About Suzy? God knows why you jumped to the conclusion that we were lovers, but I swear to you we weren't. There has never been anything like that between us.'

'If she hadn't called you darling when she rang I might not have been so jealous!' Dylan confessed.

Ross grimaced. 'She calls everyone darling! Suzy is very extrovert, extravagant, over-the-top—not my type at all.'

'What is your type?' she asked bitterly, and his fingers tightened on hers.

'You are. Don't you know that? I love your quietness—you don't talk all the time, like Suzy, or play loud pop music night and day, or chatter on the phone to friends. Alan's happy with Suzy because she suits him, but she would never suit me. I could never live with someone like that.'

She believed him now; his tone was convincing. 'She doesn't turn you on, then?' she murmured, her lashes lowered, watching him through them.

'How could you think for a second that I'd look at her when I have you?' He lifted her hand to his mouth, turned it palm upwards and softly pressed his lips into her skin, making Dylan's heart race wildly.

At that instant they heard Ruth's tread on the stairs.

'Damn, we never get a minute alone!'' muttered Ross. 'I shall be glad when we're in our own home and people can't keep walking in on us!'

So shall I, Dylan thought, still trembling from the sensual delight of having him kiss her hand.

'Here's your lunch,' Ruth said cheerfully as Ross opened the door for her.

The smell of the food made Dylan's stomach clamour—she was suddenly absolutely ravenous. How long was it since she ate anything? Breakfast seemed a long time ago. She sat up, and Ross slid pillows behind her, then Ruth placed the tray across her lap.

The casserole had a marvellous smell. It was a delight to the eye, too: golden chicken in a creamy, honey-coloured sauce, with mushrooms, slices of potato, carrot, peas and tiny herb dumplings. Ruth had brought her a glass of orange juice, too.

'I'll bring you some coffee while you eat that,' said Ruth, going out again.

'Have you eaten?' Dylan asked Ross, and he nodded.

'Ruth brought me some food a couple of hours ago.' He went back to the fire and stirred it with a long-handled brass poker, making the logs crackle and sparks fly up the chimney, little glints of red against the sooty black.

By the time Ruth came back with her coffee Dylan had finished the casserole and was leaning back against her pillows, feeling sleepy and sated.

'You were obviously starving,' Ruth laughed, taking the tray away and putting a cup of very milky coffee on the bedside table. She had brought coffee for Ross, too.

'It was delicious, thank you. I enjoyed every mouthful,' Dylan said, then with husky eagerness asked, 'Will you bring me my baby now?'

'Right away,' promised Ruth, going out, and came back at once, carrying the wicker basket she had turned into a cot, with Henry following hard on her heels.

Dylan had almost finished her coffee by then. She put the cup down and held out her arms.

'Please, bring her to me.'

'Let me,' Ross said to Ruth, who smiled indulgently at him.

Taking the baby from the basket very carefully, one hand beneath her tiny head, his other arm cradling her, Ross carried her over to the bed.

Dylan felt a tremor inside her as he put her baby into her arms. Stroking back the fine dark hair with one finger, she gazed down into the little face. Bright blue eyes stared back at her, then the baby's face turned a furious dark red, her mouth opened and she began to yell.

'What's wrong?' Ross asked, looking worried.

'She's a smart baby—she knows it's time for her first feed!' said Henry, amused. 'Dylan, your milk won't be in yet, but she'll get some nourishment from you. Let's see how you get on.'

Dylan undid the front of her cotton nightdress and uncertainly lifted the baby's small dark head to her breast, feeling the searching movements of that tiny mouth with a quiver of tenderness. Baby Ruth needed some help to get the brown-aureoled nipple between her parted lips, but once it was there she fastened on to it eagerly.

Henry smiled benignly. 'Well done!' He yawned, covering his mouth. 'Well, you obviously don't need me. I've had a long day—I'm off to bed. Goodnight.'

'If you need anything else I'll be downstairs in the kitchen for a while,'' Ruth said, going out too.

The door closed quietly. The fire was burning low again, the soft drift of the ash through the grate the only sound in the room. Dylan gazed down at her baby, gently stroking the head moving so greedily at her breast.

'Does it hurt?' asked Ross, and she smiled.

'It's a strange feeling, but not exactly painful. I think I shall enjoy feeding her.'

'She obviously enjoys it,' he murmured, staring at her naked breast. 'I can't get over the way your breasts have changed. They're twice the size they were.'

'And you hate that,' she muttered, looking at him angrily. 'I know you couldn't stand the way I looked while I was pregnant. You couldn't bear to see me, or share my bed. I turned you right off! If you'd really loved me you would never have felt like that!'

CHAPTER NINE

Ross broke out in a hoarse voice, 'Dylan, for God's sake—I told you. You aren't listening to me! I was going crazy. I didn't dare make love to you because I believed Ella—I thought she must be right, that it could be dangerous for you, or the baby, if we had sex. You're so delicate and frail; I was terrified of hurting you. I could see you were really down those last few months. You looked as if you were at the end of your tether! But believe me, darling, I wanted to make love to you so much it drove me out of my mind!'

She drew a sharp, agonising, hope-filled breath, holding that fixed, luminous stare. Did he mean it? Was that really how he had felt? Had they both been as frustrated, as unhappy, as each other?

'God knows how many nights I slept in my forest hut, freezing to death, awake half the night, but staying away from you just to stop myself getting into your bed and doing what I badly needed to do,' Ross said, his voice thickened with desire.

She said unsteadily, 'I thought you hated the way I looked!'

'I loved the way you looked. I found it intensely sexy to know my child was inside you,' he said, reaching out to touch the smooth, pale flesh of the breast his baby was sucking. 'I found it so moving, darling. I thought you were even lovelier than you had been before!'

She closed here eyes, breathing raggedly as he slowly

caressed her. 'Oh, Ross! Why didn't you tell me? If you had only said something, explained…'

'I was afraid to say anything, in case…' He was flushed, laughing. 'Well, in case one thing led to another, and I ended up doing the very thing I was determined not to do. I thought it was safer not to talk about it.' His fingers slid down to where the small mouth was clamped on her. He stroked the baby's downy cheek. 'I'd switch places with her any day!' he whispered, and Dylan laughed huskily.

The baby stopped sucking, the small head falling back, the round blue eyes staring at Ross with affront.

He laughed at her furious expression. 'Am I interrupting your dinner? Sorry, sweetheart,' he said, watching Dylan switch her to the other breast. 'She's quite a character already, isn't she?'

'She reminds me of you,' Dylan said, dimpling.

He softly pinched her ear between finger and thumb. 'Well, who else would she take after? I am her father.' His fingers pushed into Dylan's curly brown hair and he sighed. 'God—how much longer am I going to have to wait before I can make love to you, Dylan?'

She blushed and laughed. 'I don't know. I suppose it depends on how quickly I get over the birth.' That reminded her of a notice she had seen in the village a month ago. 'There are weekly aerobics classes at the village hall from January, Ross. I'll sign up for them. I can take the baby with me; they have a crêche in another room while the mothers are working out. I'll go swimming, too, and do lots more walking. That should soon get my figure back.'

His face grew serious. 'You hated being pregnant, didn't you?'

'I wanted the baby, Ross!'

'Yes, I know, but you hated being pregnant!'

She made a wry face. 'Not at first, but towards the end, when I got so heavy, I have to admit... Well, a dancer has to be light on her feet, very supple, and suddenly I was neither. I couldn't even see my feet this last couple of months!'

He smiled. 'You were never that big!'

'Oh, yes, I was—I hated seeing myself in the mirror, especially naked. That's why I found it so easy to believe you hated the sight of me, too.'

'But I didn't! Dylan, I loved seeing you heavy with my baby; you were more beautiful than ever before. Your skin glowed like a peach and you had that wonderful, smooth roundness—I was dying to touch you all the time, but I couldn't trust myself even to kiss you because I knew if I once got too close I'd never have the strength to stop myself.'

Dylan sighed, remembering the misery she had suffered during those final weeks. 'I wish you'd told me that! I know you thought you were doing the right thing, staying away from me, not making love—but you should have told me why you were being so distant, then I wouldn't have got the wrong idea. I'd have been saved a lot of grief.'

He leaned to kiss her gently, stroking her face. 'I'm sorry, Dylan, the last thing I wanted to do was hurt you. I was having a very bad time—I was eaten up with frustration and anxiety. I guess it made me very bad-tempered.'

'It certainly did! You were horrible at times! It would have made it easier if you'd talked to me about what was happening to you.'

He nodded ruefully. 'I see that now, but I'm not a great talker, I'm afraid, that's why I'm happy in my job.

I don't mind being alone for hours with nobody to talk to but my trees.'

Groaning, Dylan said, 'I think I'm more jealous of those trees than I was of Suzy! I know you love them more than me!'

'I don't love anything or anybody more than I love you, Dylan!' He let his mouth slide down her neck and she heard his breathing quicken, roughen. 'Oh, darling...you smell so wonderful.' His lips softly caressed the curve of her breast; he laid his cheek against the aching fullness their baby had just been enjoying.

Her fingers stroked his thick, warm hair which clung to her skin as if magnetically attracted. Little Ruth had fallen asleep, her head in the crook of her mother's arm, her pink lips parted in a little smile. Dylan looked down at them both, her husband, her baby, both lying against her, drifting off to sleep, and closed her own eyes with a contented look. For the first time for ages she was really happy.

Ruth woke her, and Ross, when she arrived a few minutes later and came into the room after tapping and getting no answer.

Ross sat up hurriedly, flushed and yawning. 'Sorry, I must have fallen asleep.'

Hurriedly, Dylan buttoned her nightdress bodice again with one hand while she held the baby with the other.

'All three of you were asleep. You're obviously dead tired,' Ruth said, amused. 'Ross, I've made up a bed for you in the little room across the landing; I put a hot water bottle between the sheets to warm up the bed for you. Off you go and get a good night's sleep.'

He stood up, stretching with a yawn. 'That sounds wonderful. I hardly slept at all last night, or the night before—I must be running on the last of my adrenalin.'

'I'm sure you are,' nodded Ruth. 'Give me the baby, Dylan. She can sleep in the room with me, downstairs, then I can change her or give her a bottle, if she wakes up during the night. I want you to try and sleep again, but if you need me all you have to do is yell. I'm a light sleeper; I'll hear you.'

'You can leave her here. I can cope—I'll have to once I get home with her,' Dylan protested as Ruth picked up the wicker basket.

'No, after all the effort of the birth you need a good rest. Doesn't she, Ross?'

'Yes,' he obediently agreed. 'Ruth's right. Goodnight, darling. See you in the morning.'

Giving her a kiss on top of her head, he went out, and Ruth took the baby very carefully, trying not to wake her. As she laid the child in the wicker basket little Ruth stirred, frowning petulantly, grizzled a little, then yawned and went back to sleep as Ruth carried her out of the room.

Ruth slept fitfully that night, woken up several times by the crying of the baby. At first light she was up, walking the kitchen floor, with the baby over her shoulder, red-faced and hiccuping with wind after a bottle, the tiny fists clenched and flailing impotently.

'Shhh…shhhh…' soothed Ruth, patting the baby's back, and when that didn't work tried singing a lullaby she remembered from her own childhood, although she only remembered some of the words. She filled in the rest with humming wordlessly, and the baby quietened, listening.

'That isn't a bad voice. You should be in the church choir,' Henry said from the door, making her jump and swing round to face him.

He had washed and shaved, brushed smooth his white hair and was clear-eyed and smiling, a warm blue sweater she recognised as one of her own worn casually over the shirt he had worn yesterday. Seeing her look at it, he grinned. 'You don't mind my borrowing this, do you? I was cold when I first got up.'

'Of course not. I'm amazed it fits you so well—you might as well keep it. I never wear it, but it suits you.'

'Well, thank you, and a Happy Christmas!'

'Oh, my God, I'd forgotten it was Christmas,' she groaned, horrified by the lapse of memory.

'How could you forget that with a Christmas baby in your arms?' he teased, laughing. 'And a house full of Christmas guests! What are you going to give us all for lunch today? I don't smell a turkey cooking in the range, and there's no sign of a Christmas pudding waiting to boil!'

Ruth grimaced at him. 'I wasn't intending to bother about Christmas. There's no point when you live alone.'

Henry gazed at her, face becoming serious. 'I know how you feel. I didn't bother to make any preparations, either. I sent a few cards and bought a few presents, but I didn't bother to put up decorations or a tree. I had any number of invitations.'

Yes, thought Ruth a little acidly, he didn't need to tell her that. She could imagine who from! There were several women without a man in the village who had their eyes on him; he was still very attractive, despite his white hair, rugged, forceful. An eligible divorcee with a nice house of his own and plenty of money, he had no need to spend Christmas alone.

There had been no such invitations for her. Who wanted a dull, greying old spinster hanging about over the festive season, when families came together again and people tried to forget all their worries, to shut out the rest of the world, have fun and be happy?

'Whose invitation did you accept?' she asked, aware that the baby had fallen asleep over her shoulder, the small body heavy in that wonderful abandonment which could be so touching.

'Yours,' Henry murmured, looking amused.

Her eyes widened. 'I didn't invite you!'

'No, but here I am, and I might as well stay for the rest of the day. Why don't I make coffee while you take that baby upstairs to its mother? Then we can cook a Christmas breakfast together while we work out how we can make this a very special day for our unexpected visitors.'

He seemed different today. His mood was light-hearted, and that bitter tang which had darkened his voice, his face, ever since his wife left him seemed to have gone.

'You seem very cheerful,' she almost accused.

'It's called the Christmas spirit,' Henry said. 'And if you aren't careful, when you get back from delivering that child to its mother I may have found some mistletoe!'

Ruth was appalled to find herself blushing to the roots of her hair. 'Don't talk daft!' she muttered, moving towards the door with the baby over her shoulder.

'Daft, am I? Well, for that, if I can't find any mistletoe I'll do without. You don't need mistletoe to snatch a kiss!'

His grin was wicked; his eyes gleamed with warm amusement.

Ruth hurriedly left the room, feeling oddly breathless. She had never dared admit to herself how strong her feelings were for Henry. You're too old to dream, she had always told herself. Don't be so stupid. He's married, anyway. Are you out of your mind?

She had almost managed to fool herself into believing she thought of Henry as just a friend—but she had never fooled his wife. Gwen had been far too shrewd, not to mention a woman with a poisonous tongue and a mind like a steel trap.

Embarrassed, humiliated, Ruth would have died rather than admit Gwen was right. She'd been terrified Gwen had told him, appalled at the thought that he might guess how she felt. Ever since that day when Gwen had accused her of chasing Henry, Ruth had put on a polite, friendly but offhand mask with him.

Even when Gwen ran off with her toy boy Ruth had gone on trying to convince Henry that all she felt was friendship towards him, nothing more, and Henry's own humiliation and bitterness had made it easy.

Suddenly their relationship had altered—she didn't know why or when.

Ross was already awake and out of bed. For a second when his eyes had flicked open he hadn't remembered where he was; the tiny box room was shadowy, although the sun rising outside flashed glittering reflections of snow on to the ceiling. As his memory had brought him up to speed he'd sat up, jumped out of bed, and put on the well-washed old dressing gown Ruth had found for him last night. It was rather short on him and he felt ridiculous.

When he carefully opened Dylan's door the room was empty. The bedclothes were flung back but no sign of Dylan.

His heart stopped, then began to race in panic. Where was she? Where was the baby?

Then the bathroom door opened and Dylan appeared, wearing a long, lemon-coloured cotton nightie which blew back against her, outlining the round breasts, small waist and slim hips in a way that went straight to Ross's head. Seeing him, she stopped to look at him, her blue eyes wide before she smiled, a tremulous, quivering smile that touched him so deeply he didn't even smile back, just looked at her passionately.

'Hello.' His voice was deep, husky.

'Hello,' she said, in a shy little-girl murmur, as if they were total strangers, and limped towards the bed.

He hadn't noticed any limp yesterday; he stiffened. 'What have you done? Why are you limping?'' He followed her across the room.

Climbing into bed, Dylan pulled the covers up over herself and sat up against the pillows. 'I hurt my ankle when I crashed, but it's getting better already; it was just a sprain.'

'Let me see.'

She pushed her foot out from under the bedclothes and he gingerly inspected it, his fingers gentle.

'It looks painful—does it hurt much?'

'Only when I walk. The swelling is going down now.'

'Has Henry seen it?'

'Of course!' She drew her foot back under the covers. 'He said it wasn't serious and would soon heal.' Changing the subject, she asked him, 'Did you sleep well?'

'I must have done. I don't remember a thing after I put out the light until I woke up a few minutes ago.' He sat on the edge of her bed to kiss her lingeringly. 'Mmm…you've had a shower. Your skin is damp and smells flowery.'

Dylan suddenly realised he had slept naked. His dress-

ing gown had fallen open over his legs and she could
see the rough hair on his bare thigh. Her breathing was
suddenly faster, ragged with excitement. Ross glanced
down to see what she was staring at and inhaled sharply.
Taking one of her hands, he placed it on his thigh,
watching her with a burning desire in his dark grey eyes.

Dylan's fingers slid upward over the short dark curls
of hair, touched him intimately, feeling his flesh harden
and stir; he shut his eyes, groaning her name.

'It's been so long...'

'Too long,' she whispered.

Neither of them had heard Ruth coming up the stairs.
Luckily a stair on the landing creaked loudly before she
walked into the room. Dylan had time to snatch her hand
back, and Ross hurriedly stood up, dragging his dressing
gown together while his back was towards the door.
They were both red and breathing fast.

'Here's Mummy,' Ruth told the baby, carrying her
over to Dylan. 'I said you would see her in a minute,
didn't I? Say Happy Christmas!'

'Christmas!' repeated Ross, taken aback. 'I'd forgotten all about it!'

Holding out her arms, Dylan took the child, smiling
into those wide, staring blue eyes.

'Hello, darling. Happy Christmas to you, too—did
you sleep all night?'

'She was very good,' Ruth lied. 'A real Christmas
angel.'

Dylan ran a finger down the baby's cheek. 'She smells
so nice!' Then she noticed the clothes the baby was
wearing and blinked in surprise. 'Where did you get
those?' The dress was a faded blue gingham with lacy
cuffs and collar, and looked a little odd but rather sweet
on the baby, especially as it was rather short on her

dimpled legs. On top of that the baby was wearing a tiny blue knitted cardigan of a curiously old-fashioned design.

Ruth laughed. 'I stole them.'

'Stole them?' Dylan repeated, wide-eyed.

'I never throw anything away,' Ruth admitted. 'I still have most of my old toys in the little box room, including two dolls with china faces and soft bodies. I know it's daft...'

'Of course it isn't,' Dylan contradicted, smiling at her. 'I've kept a couple of my own dolls, and my old teddy, although he's very battered and has lost an eye.'

'I'm glad I'm not the only sentimental idiot!' Ruth laughed. 'While I was getting the room ready for your husband yesterday, I realised my dolls were the same size as the baby, so I took their clothes off and washed and tumbled-dried them. I left them in front of the range all night, and put them on the baby after I bathed her just now—they fit her perfectly. I think my mother must have used some of my old baby clothes to dress my dolls after she bought them.'

'Recycling with a vengeance,' said Ross, laughing. 'How wonderful. She looks adorable in them, too.' He ran a hand over the baby's head. 'Look at all that hair! I had the idea babies were born bald.'

'Some are, according to Henry.' Ruth turned her head, sniffing. 'I smell bacon and coffee. I'll leave the baby with you, Dylan. What do you fancy for breakfast? Egg and bacon? Fruit and cereal? Coffee or tea?'

'Whatever you're having, thank you.'

'Okay. How about you, Ross?'

'I'll have the same, too, thanks. This is really very kind of you, Ruth. It must be a nuisance having your Christmas ruined this way.'

'It isn't being ruined! I can't remember the last time I enjoyed Christmas this much,' Ruth said, smiling as she went back downstairs.

'What a nice woman,' Ross said, about to sit down on the bed again. But Dylan shooed him away.

'Go and have a shower before breakfast. You haven't much time, judging by that gorgeous smell of bacon!'

He went, laughing but reluctant, and Dylan cradled her baby, moved by the feel of her small, warm body. 'You're beautiful, do you know that?'

The dark blue eyes gazed up at her.

'Yes, you do know, don't you?' Dylan laughed, kissing the tiny button nose. 'Hungry? Yes, I thought you would be.'

She opened her nightdress.

Ruth brought up her breakfast on a tray half an hour later and found the baby fast asleep, pink and contented, in her mother's arms.

'Give her to me. I'll take her back downstairs and put her into the basket. Is feeding her getting any easier?'

'She seems to enjoy it; that's the main thing. What are you putting in her bottle, Ruth? Cow's milk?'

'No, Henry very thoughtfully brought along some more powdered feed, a couple of bottles and some sterilising tablets on his last run. Not to mention some disposable nappies, which make life much easier. Now, you eat your breakfast, then you can have a nap.'

Dylan looked at the bran flakes with sliced banana, the covered plate of bacon and egg, the toast and coffee.

'It all looks marvellous, and I am starving, but if I keep eating like this I shall be even fatter than when I was pregnant!' she moaned.

'You can't diet while you're breastfeeding,' said Ruth, taking the baby out and closing the door.

After she had eaten her breakfast and put the tray on the floor Dylan lay back, sunlight on her closed lids, in a trance of happiness.

Downstairs Ruth put the baby into her wicker basket in the sunny sitting room while Cleo watched, slit eyes bright green.

'It's a baby,' Ruth told her. 'And you stay away from it, do you hear me?' She covered the baby and shooed Cleo out of the room, closing the door firmly.

Tail lashing in affront, Cleo walked off into the kitchen and curled up in a patch of sunlight on the mat, from where she could see Fred mooching around the garden, gloomily looking for green things poking through the blanket of white snow.

Henry was talking on the mobile phone. 'Well, that's a wonder! If there are any emergencies, I shall be here all day at Ruth's cottage. Oh, and Meg... Happy Christmas!'

He switched off and met Ruth's questioning stare. 'My message service,' he explained. 'Nobody needs me so far, touch wood. No really serious problems have come up overnight. Look, Ross and I are going off to see what we can scavenge to make this a real Christmas. We may be gone an hour or so, but apparently the temperature is rising again and there's a thaw on the way, so we're unlikely to run into any difficulty.'

'The shops will all be shut! And anyway, I found a very big chicken in my deep freeze. I've been thawing it out in the microwave; I'll start cooking it in half an hour.'

Henry wagged a finger at her. 'The village store will open up for me! Jack has been a patient of mine for donkey's years; he owes me a favour. Start cooking your chicken; I'll bring back whatever else I can find.'

While they were gone Ruth prepared the chicken, stuffing it with a mixture of the herbs she grew on her windowsill and some chestnuts she had in her larder. She had meant to roast them whole, in their skins, instead she peeled them, then chopped them up very small. Before she put the bird into the oven she pushed a whole unpeeled orange into the mouth of the cavity to give a faintly orangey flavour to the meat, then laid strips of bacon criss-cross over the top.

By the time Henry and Ross returned the whole house was full of the scent of roasting chicken.

The two men stamped their boots on the mat before coming indoors, faces healthily flushed after their tussle with the wind, smelling of fresh, cold air, and bringing waves of it in with them.

Each of them carried a couple of carrier bags, but they refused to let Ruth see the contents of all the bags. Ross vanished into the sitting room with the two he carried, but Henry put his bags on the kitchen table.

'These are full of food. You can unpack them and see what a treasure trove we found!' Henry announced proudly.

Her face lit up as she saw that they had managed to get a Christmas pudding, a string bag of walnuts, almonds and hazelnuts, a small Christmas cake, biscuits, fruit, half a dozen cartons of milk and several of orange juice.

'That's marvellous,' Ruth said gratefully to Henry, as he helped her put everything into cupboards.

'I checked what you had in your larder before we went, to make sure I didn't buy stuff you already had—you didn't intend to have Christmas at all, did you?'

'Any more than you did,' she drily told him.

He grimaced. 'True—but, do you know? I'm enjoying it for the first time in years. How about you?'

She nodded, smiling. 'I'm having a wonderful time.'

Henry put his hand into his trouser pocket and produced something green; he held it over her head, leaned down and kissed her on her startled lips.

Eyes wide and bright, Ruth recklessly threw her arms around his neck and kissed him back.

Then, flushed and laughing, they looked at each other as if neither had ever really seen the other before.

'Happy Christmas, Ruth!' he said, warmth and gentleness in his face, and she happily echoed the words.

'Happy Christmas, Henry.'

He took a deep, audible breath, then plunged on, 'I don't suppose you'd consider marrying me?'

Ruth didn't believe her ears; lips parted in a gasp of shock, she gazed back at him for a second or two, almost made some shy, embarrassed response which might have frozen them both for another year or two, then threw modesty to the winds and huskily said, 'Yes! Oh, yes, Henry!'

Ross carried Dylan, in her nightie and dressing gown, downstairs just after two o'clock. 'Don't drop me, will you?' she said, a little nervously, both arms around his neck as he picked her up from the bed. 'Are you sure I won't be too heavy for you?'

He hoisted her closer to him, the soft folds of her clothes trailing over his arm. 'Now you've had the baby you're as light as a feather again! And more beautiful than you ever were!'

She hid her face in his throat, her mouth pressing into him. 'Flatterer!'

At the foot of the stairs, he said, 'Now, close your eyes!'

'Why?'

'We've got a surprise for you!'

Laughing, she shut her eyes, and Ross walked through the door of the sitting room. Dylan inhaled a familiar scent of pine, reminding her of the forest around their home.

'You can look now!' he told her, and she opened her eyes, blinking in the dazzle of coloured lights on a very tall Christmas tree.

'Oh! How lovely!' Dylan gazed in delight at the fairy lights, winking on and off, red and blue and gold among the dark green branches.

A silver tinsel star was perched on top of the tree and there was a little pile of wrapped gifts underneath. The room was hung with glittering gold and red tinsel chains which reflected the dancing firelight in the hearth, in front of which stood Henry and Ruth, watching her, flushed and smiling.

'Ross did it all himself,' Ruth said. 'He even found some holly, with a few berries on it!'

'And some mistletoe,' said Henry,. 'A happy Christmas, Dylan.' He held a bottle of champagne in one hand, a glass in the other. He poured a glass, bubbles winking at the brim, while Ross carefully put Dylan into a chair in front of the fire. Henry handed her the glass of champagne, saying, 'Before we have lunch we thought we would drink to you two and your baby. You've made this the best Christmas either of us can remember—a Christmas we'll never forget!'

'We're going to be married, Dylan,' Ruth said huskily, very pink and shy, looking years younger.

'Oh, how marvellous. I'm so glad!' Dylan glowed with delight.

Ross looked stunned for a few seconds, then he recovered, smiling, and raised the glass of champagne Henry had just given him. 'What great news. Congratulations, both of you. Henry, you're a lucky man. You'll be getting a wife nearly as wonderful as mine. I hope you'll both be very happy.'

'We will be,' Henry firmly told him. 'I should have got around to proposing to her long ago, but I was always so busy, and I'm a slow thinker. It wasn't until I saw her looking after Dylan and the baby that I realised just how I felt about her. She's one in a million, and I'm grabbing her while I have the chance.'

Ruth laughed. 'I'm grabbing you, too. At our age we can't afford to waste any more time.'

'We won't. And stop talking as if we're old; we're not—we've got the best years of our lives ahead of us!' he assured her. 'We'll have to sit down and plan our honeymoon tomorrow. We'll go somewhere neither of us has ever been. When you're starting life over again you should grab every new experience you can!'

She laughed, flushed and excited.

'We owe both of you an enormous debt,' Ross said, sitting down on the arm of Dylan's chair. 'We're very grateful. We can never thank you enough for what you did for us.'

'You've already repaid us,' Henry said. 'If Dylan hadn't crashed her car out there we might have gone on for years without realising how much we needed each other. She changed our lives.'

Dylan and Ruth smiled silently at each other as their men talked, then Ruth gave an exclamation. 'The roast potatoes! They'll be burnt black if I don't get them out soon! Excuse me, won't you?'

She hurried out of the room. Henry said, 'She'll need some help—sorry. You two finish your champagne. We'll give you a shout when lunch is ready.'

As he went out Ross looked down at Dylan, amusement in his eyes. 'How about that bombshell, then? Who'd have expected that?'

'Me,' she said firmly. 'It was as clear as day to me that Ruth loved him, and she's such a darling. I was just afraid he would never get round to realising what a great wife she would be.'

'Why do women always have to know everything?' Ross asked drily, then glanced up at the ceiling. 'See where I put your chair?'

Dylan threw a look upwards, saw the piece of mistletoe suspended over her head, and gave him a teasing look. 'Opportunist!'

He leaned down to kiss her, one hand softly stroking her neck and the full curve of her breast. 'I love you, darling,' he whispered against her yielding mouth.

The baby in her basket slept. In the kitchen and in the sitting room lovers kissed. Outside in a blue sky the sun shone over snowy fields and trees like crystal. Indoors, the Christmas tree lights gleamed, red flames blazed up the chimney; there was a nostalgic scent of oranges, nuts, pine and holly and the air was full of anticipation.

HARLEQUIN ⬥ PRESENTS®

EXPECTING!

She's sexy, she's successful... and she's pregnant!

Relax and enjoy these new stories about spirited women and gorgeous men, whose passion results in pregnancies... sometimes unexpectedly! All the new parents-to-be will discover that the business of making babies brings with it the most special love of all....

If you enjoyed what you just read,
then we've got an offer you can't resist!

Take 2 bestselling
love stories FREE!
Plus get a FREE surprise gift!

EXTRA! EXTRA!

**The book all your favorite authors
are raving about is finally here!**

The 1999 Harlequin and Silhouette
coupon book.

**Each page is alive with savings that can't be beat!
Getting this incredible coupon book is
as easy as 1, 2, 3.**

1. During the months of November and December 1999 buy any 2 Harlequin or Silhouette books.

2. Send us your name, address and 2 proofs of purchase (cash receipt) to the address below.

3. Harlequin will send you a coupon book worth $10.00 off future purchases of Harlequin or Silhouette books in 2000.

Send us 3 cash register receipts as proofs of purchase and we will send you 2 coupon books worth a total saving of $20.00 (limit of 2 coupon books per customer).

Saving money has never been this easy.

Please allow 4-6 weeks for delivery. Offer expires December 31, 1999.

I accept your offer! Please send me (a) coupon booklet(s):

Name: _____

Address: _____ City: _____

State/Prov.: _____ Zip/Postal Code: _____

Send your name and address, along with your cash register receipts as proofs of purchase, to:

In the U.S.: Harlequin Books, P.O. Box 9057, Buffalo, N.Y. 14269

In Canada: Harlequin Books, P.O. Box 622, Fort Erie, Ontario L2A 5X3

Order your books and accept this coupon offer through our web site
http://www.romance.net
Valid in U.S. and Canada only.

PHQ4994R

HARLEQUIN PRESENTS®

Seduction
SWEET REVENGE

They wanted to get even.
Instead they got...married!

by bestselling author

Penny Jordan

Don't miss Penny Jordan's latest enthralling miniseries about four special women. Kelly, Anna, Beth and Dee share a bond of friendship and a burning desire to avenge a wrong. But in their quest for revenge, they each discover an even stronger emotion.
Love.

Look out for all four books in Harlequin Presents®:

November 1999
THE MISTRESS ASSIGNMENT

December 1999
LOVER BY DECEPTION

January 2000
A TREACHEROUS SEDUCTION

February 2000
THE MARRIAGE RESOLUTION

Available at your favorite retail outlet.

HARLEQUIN®
Makes any time special ™

HARLEQUIN ◆ PRESENTS®

*invites you to see
how the other half marry in:*

SOCIETY WEDDINGS

This sensational new five-book miniseries invites
you to be our VIP guest at some of the most talked-
about weddings of the decade—spectacular events
where the cream of society gather to celebrate the
marriages of dazzling brides and grooms in
breathtaking, international locations.

Be there to toast each of the happy couples:

Aug. 1999—**The Wedding-Night Affair**, #2044,
Miranda Lee

Sept. 1999—**The Impatient Groom**, #2054,
Sara Wood

Oct. 1999—**The Mistress Bride**, #2056,
Michelle Reid

Nov. 1999—**The Society Groom**, #2066,
Mary Lyons

Dec. 1999—**A Convenient Bridegroom**, #2067,
Helen Bianchin

Available wherever Harlequin books are sold.

HARLEQUIN®
Makes any time special ™